URBAN VOODOO

Edgardo Cozarinsky

Preface by Susan Sontag

"The Sentimental Journey"
translated by Ronald Christ and the Author

Lumen Books
446 West 20 Street
New York, NY 10011
(212) 989-7944

ISBN 0-930829-15-8

Printed in the United States of America
First American Edition

Lumen Books are produced by Lumen, Inc., a tax-exempt, non-profit organization. This publication is made possible, in part, with public funds from the New York State Council on the Arts, the National Endowment for the Arts, and private contributions.

Cover photograph: Dennis L. Dollens

For Sara. For Miron.

THE EXILE'S COSMOPOLIS

Susan Sontag

Urban Voodoo is an exile's book. An eminently cosmopolitan—therefore, transnational—book. And yet, in its proud bookishness and its self-conscious relation to the notion of a native language, it seems very Argentine—Argentina being something of a transnational country, with its chronically displaced cultural ideals administered by an Anglophile upper class and generations of Paris-based writers and artists. The modernist tradition of Argentine letters has been gleefully erudite, fanciful, rigged: literature about literature, which presumes the universal library. The greatest Spanish-language writer of our time was an Argentine who learned to read English before Spanish, and read *Don Quixote* first in an English translation; who, though he decided to become Jorge Luis Borges instead of George Borges, never stopped insisting that he was an epigone of English literature.

Cozarinsky is a late Borgesian whose presiding literary models are—with the exception of Borges—not Spanish either, but French, German, Russian, and who has taken even further the principle of linguistic duplicity and the art of cultural displacement. *Urban Voodoo* is a displaced book first of all in that it does not have a single "original" language. Only the first part, "The Sentimental Journey," was written in the author's native Spanish. (I can't help hearing in this title a displaced homage to the author of the single most influential work of English literature upon modernist Spanish-language, as well as Eastern and Central European writers—*Tristram Shandy*.) The second part of his book, as Cozarinsky explains in a note at the end, was written in a language he calls "foreigner's English." Although expertly trilingual, he is not one of the tiny number of linguistic virtuosos like Beckett, Nabokov, and Cabrera Infante, who write equally (and ardently) well in two or more languages. The literary appeal to Cozarinsky of his second and third languages, English and French, is partly the degree to which they retain the sediment, the impurities of foreignness.

Urban Voodoo belongs to several strong modern meta-genres. One, the older, is the rueful, semi-hallucinatory depiction of the irreducible strangeness of modern city life. Another is the treatise on exile. The urban promenades of the refined solitary consciousness used to be mainly a form of slumming. But since the moral opprobrium attached to savoring kitsch and to seeking instant sex has been lightened, the contemporary *flâneur* no longer has "low" experiences —merely "fast" ones. The standard literary form for the consumer of fast experiences, experiences that one passes through, is the postcard, which is what Cozarinsky calls the short units of his book. Not stories but postcards—the tourist's screed.

Besides these ironies something else is suggested by *postcard*: that a postcard is usually both word and image. Like a film. Cozarinsky, who is a filmmaker turned writer, or a writer turned filmmaker, has produced here an album of postcards made of words only. But his postcards might well take visual form; indeed, the possibilty is already adumbrated in the boldest sequences of his first (fiction) film, made in Buenos Aires, *Dot Dot Dot*, and his recent montage-film, *One Man's War*, about Nazi-occupied Paris.

The writer's sensibility has been, it seems fair to assume, reinforced by that of the filmmaker formed in the era of Godard. Like Godard, who said he wanted to make fiction films that are like documentaries and documentaries that are like fiction films, Cozarinsky wants to write (autobiographical) stories that are like essays, essays that are like stories. His lavish use of quotations in the form of epigraphs reminds me of the quotation-strewn films of Godard. In the sense that Godard the cinéphile director makes films out of, and about, his romance with movies, Cozarinsky has made a book out of, and about, his romance with certain books. Some of these evocations of a phantasmagorical city are prose poems, like Baudelaire's *Le Spleen de Paris*; some are novels, like Biely's *Petersburg*, or prose fantasias, like Breton's *Nadja* and Aragon's *Le Paysan de Paris*; some are essays, like the ruminations on the arcades and big department stores of Paris by Walter Benjamin—the Benjamin inspired by Baudelaire and the Surrealists; the connoisseur of montage and of quotations.

Cozarinsky's Buenos Aires (the local past) and Paris (the

cosmopolitan present) are both capitals of retroactive as well as anticipated longing. The vulgar or illicit avidities and carnal achievements of the contemporary *flâneur* are largely a mental transaction, a kind of lived literature (or cinema). While the modern city continues to be an emporium of desires, these impure enchantments are saturated with a foretaste of their own finitude. All the more need, then, for the writer's voodoo: by conjuring up the past, to heighten unappeased desires and also to exorcise them.

Last night, looking for an x-ray that he had obviously mislaid, he spent almost an hour buried in a box full of papers that had rarely seen the light of day: a monotonous jumble of gas and electricity bills, train schedules, and publicity brochures for hotels. Among them he found an airline ticket that he automatically set aside: he thought he would file it later, along with some papers that, with more luck than cunning, might earn him a tax deduction. Abandoning hope, he finally returned all of them to their common purgatory, just as he had done more than once over the years, without daring to find them a new, temporary home in the garbage can.

A quick glance told him the ticket was too old to be worth any refund and also revealed the last page, still unused, in the folder. Only then did he realize, with a jab sharp and stabbing as an electric shock, that this was the ticket on which "he had gone away": the last page corresponded to the never-taken return of a round-trip Buenos Aires/Paris flight, paid in advance.

Like the memory of a disease overcome long ago, he recalled the scruples of his prudent attitude—crusts and crumbs of a sensible education, fears and tremblings of an identity now cast off: even at the moment of making a distressing decision in the face of impending chaos, he was capable of investing (what at that time seemed) a considerable sum in order to assure himself of the possibility of returning: "just in case . . ."

Paris-Buenos Aires. Open. Tourist Class. Baggage limit: 20 kg. Not valid after . . .

Yes, almost a year after buying it, already knowing he was not going back (even though he had never made the decision: as so often happens, he had reached what others could see all along as a final decision through a series of trifling, almost imperceptible gestures), he visited the Paris office of the airline to see if he could get his money back or exchange the last page for the equivalent mileage in another direction. With unshakable courtesy, the clerk explained: the unrelenting devaluation of Argentine currency (this conversation must have taken place around the end of '75) necessitated the airline's enforcing a strict policy of no conversions. It took him a moment to translate such jargon and realize that they would not refund his money in the strong dollars (required by the International Organization of Air Carriers) that the ticket had cost him, but only in the amount of *pesos*, very weak by then, he had needed to buy those dollars . . . Hours later, from a long distance call to his mother, he learned that this amount, only months after he purchased the ticket, would scarcely buy him a pair of shoes in Buenos Aires, or, well, an album, not to be sneered at, of three cassettes: *Great Ladies in the History of the Tango*.

Without emotion, with a certain curiosity about the former person the ticket seemed to reveal in some way, he examined the folder, or, rather, its single remaining page. For a second he recognized one of his reflections in a museum archivist's temptation to frame it . . . But his old superstitious self won out: moments later he watched the remains of the ticket disappear, among flames and ashes, down the toilet.

Later that same night, he paused in his work and looked out the window.

The corner *tabac* was still noisy and full, even though all the other lights on the street had gone out: not even its fuchsia-colored neon lozenge was visible. After redoubling his effort, without great conviction, to get on with a translation into Spanish of Leiris—*Literature Considered as Bullfighting*—he gave in and accepted the fact that he really wanted to go out for a drink.

It was one of those pleasant evenings so rare in Paris, when the heat of the day, relieved by a cool breeze, lets you stay out on the sidewalk, seated at a café table in your shirt-sleeves, well after midnight. The corner *tabac* seemed unusually lively for the 20th *arrondissement*. Its voices, its noises—cranky but vague—assaulted him like a radio turned up too loud. Only after not being able to find a place outside and hesitantly standing in the doorway did he notice the considerable renovation the place had undergone. Gone, for instance, were the intricate neon lights, vanished, like the gleaming copper bar, the wooden-top tables, and, over the cash register, the painted white letters that announced on the mirror a *plat du jour* that did not change every day.

The place looked renovated, for sure, in a style of shiny formica and indirect lighting. But it also seemed familiar, in some way he could not put his finger on. Something suggested a clue: the lighted sign over the door no longer advertised Stella Artois, Queen of Beers, but Alabama Coffee and Teas, a brand apparently well on the way to replacing the café's original name, still visible, but just barely, on the dark wall where the electric sign hung. Behind the neon, you could still make out, across four green leaves of a painted-over emblem, the words *El Trébol*.

He was struck by disbelief, brief but more intense than these lines I'm writing, perhaps even greater than the most admirable syntactic feat. Stunned, dumbfounded, he yielded to the suspension of his disbelief: out came Guillermo, smiling, to greet him with a hug, to lead him, as if enveloped in his hug, toward a car parked at the corner.

"Just like you, to come back without letting anybody know . . . Doesn't matter, you're discovered: you're *found out*!" With open hands he sweeps the air left to right as if to describe the size of shocking headlines in an afternoon tabloid.

"We thought about you so much last fall . . . Elisa and I were in Paris for a week, we wanted to give you a ring, somebody'd given us your number, must've been Emilio, but, as it turned out you weren't at that number anymore." His arms close around the rediscovered friend: "Great to see you again!"

He mumbles something, approximative words, that may not distract him, engrossed as he is in the magnitude of the set and in the dazzling lighting effects it must have taken hundreds of veteran electricians to set up in just a few seconds: all of Santa Fe Avenue spreads out before the Mercedes convertible, the lights reflecting over its shiny body (in the best tradition of "night in the city" movies) while the car moves through numberless extras, who, with a carefree manner, cover the sidewalks or sit at café tables in the warmth of an evening he has finally recognized.

"Let's go home and surprise Elisa. We have to have a drink

to celebrate." For a moment he forgets his unconvincing responses. He feels no need to justify the fact of his being here, as if the effort to cover his bewilderment had simply wiped it out. He improvises some remarks to indicate—his excitement? his enthusiasm? He finds clichés, sincere nonetheless, to say that Guillermo hasn't changed a bit (while in the rearview mirror he comes face to face with his baldness, the creases that line his eyes) before slipping into one of those omnivorous questions of the "How's things?" type, almost unavoidable after years of being spared the exchange of daily trivia.

Guillermo does not seem to notice.

"You weren't home, at the new place, were you? Of course not, I forgot you left so long ago: I don't know, doesn't seem real . . . We moved last year. It's great for the kids—knock on wood—that the terrace and the pool keep them from wanting to go out on the street. You're not going to recognize them: Mariano's eleven already, María Marta seven. But I want to know what you're up to, you're not going to get away with not telling us. I know you write, also that . . . The title escapes me . . . They showed one of your films at the Cannes Festival, right? We read about it in the paper. Great!"

The spectacle of the city is so hypnotic that he does not manage an answer. Everything he used to recall for years is there, everything faithfully reproduced down to the last detail, and the result is the deceptive lifelikeness of a dream, disturbing in the way a hyper-realistic animated cartoon could be . . . But maybe Guillermo was not expecting him to answer. He guesses from his friend's greeting that he expects a predictable character. He cannot even tell what part he is supposed to play, so better tread carefully and not step outside the chalk marks laid down for him. Guillermo smiles and a shade of melancholy politeness colors his voice:

"You don't know how I envy you every time I think about you . . . Yes, though that may seem strange to you. You're doing everything you wanted to, you're working at what you like, you don't answer to anybody, you're your own boss. You're living the life of an artist!"

At last! He finally finds the part he has been cast in, there is no more need to fill in the blanks. Relieved, he understands he does not have to confess that he does not know how to pay next month's rent if he also pays the phone bill . . . Does Guillermo suspect? Could it matter? He tries to improvise a line, some comment that will be true and at the same time neither humiliating to himself nor condescending to Guillermo. But they are already at Libertador, they have passed the Museo de Bellas Artes, and they come to a stop in front of a tall apartment building that was not there when he went away.

As Guillermo smiles at the TV monitor in the lobby, he takes advantage of this momentary silence to tell him that a few weeks ago the London *Times* movie critic had recalled with pleasure Guillermo's first, and up to now only, film—shown at a festival eight years ago. He gets no answer and is already piling on more small talk—that out of sight's not out of mind—when Guillermo speaks again.

"Elisa's going to be surprised!"

He has not spoken like someone interrupting somebody else, nor does he seem to notice that he has cut his friend short. Rather, he speaks as though nobody had been talking. Didn't he hear him? They are standing one in front of the other in the elevator . . .

"We're here!" Guillermo announces when the door slides back with a gentle whir to reveal the understated entrance to a penthouse.

Elisa responds immediately to the "Guess who's here": she enters and rushes over to hug him. He recognizes her only at that instant: he had seen her often during those incredible late '60s, almost certainly when she "danced to silence" at the Instituto di Tella. (He also recalls that during those days she was married to a free-jazz musician, declared a *desaparecido* a few years later.) If anything, she looks younger, almost diaphanous, and her hair, though cut short, has the same reddish-chestnut highlights he remembers.

"You must tell me everything," she whispers in his ear as they embrace, almost like making a secret date with him.

His daze subsides, he starts feeling comfortable. They listen to him, they flatter him. His confidence grows. He recounts. What? No obscene poverty, of course; at most, some doubts, an occasional uncertainty. Undismayed, they smile, making him feel they really understand how he feels, greatly appreciate his frankness. Elisa takes the plunge first.

"But . . . isn't that the privilege, let's say the luxury, of living in Paris? There you can be . . . well . . . poor?"

Guillermo steps on her line.

"Come on, come on. You know perfectly well he never really tried to, he never really was interested in making money." Their smiles broaden and stiffen, their eyes grow brighter, their glance more penetrating. "That's why we love you so much!"

Behind one large window the city's lights punctuate the darkness as far as the eye can see; behind the other, the river stretches, peaceful, silent, beneath a full moon. He has touched a sore spot, which reacts to the contact, and he pulls back. At the foot of the curtains, almost smothered in the hairy Finnish rug, a doll the size of a five-year-old girl looks at him spitefully. "My name is Miami Lulu and I speak Spanish. What's yours?" Astonished, he is on the verge of answering when he gets hold of himself and starts laughing. Elisa smiles but doesn't seem amused.

"That frightful thing! All her schoolmates have one and I had no way of dissuading her . . ."

She gestures vaguely with impatience. Guillermo comes to her rescue with exactly the right words.

"We have to toast the traveller returned."

They are back in the car, going along Libertador. A breeze, which seems intoxicating, strikes him in the face. Suddenly he realizes that, in different periods, both Guillermo and Elisa knew Marcos. He asks if they know what has happened to him. The last he knew, Marcos's mother had gone to see an archbishop who had good contacts in the army and suggested that maybe Marcos was not dead but serving an indeterminate sentence in a prison camp in Córdoba. But that was already two years ago and there has been no news since.

They have stopped at a dangerous intersection, waiting for the light to change. Other cars honk their horns, and his friends do not hear him. Starting up again, a moment later, they have already forgotten his question.

Now, surrounded by a chattering crowd, they are sipping Blue Lagoons under striped canvas awnings, somewhere amid blocks of sidewalks covered with open-air tables. A rainbow of spotlights shining on the tree trunks drenches them in blaring technicolor.

"Oh, my God, my senior partner is over there," Guillermo smothers a groan.

Elisa shows her sensible side: "Isn't it better to say hello and face up to him?"

"Sure," Guillermo murmurs, but he does not turn his head or get up. Instead he offers a glimpse into professional life: "Tomorrow I have to show him the first ad in the Purring Purina campaign. I saw it a couple of hours ago and, well, I frankly don't think it's what we want."

In solidarity with him, Elisa prompts a worried look. He gets the hint and tries to put one on. Silence descends for a few seconds, shrouding them, the void filled by disco music (from a neighboring jukebox? from a car parked nearby?) . . . He listens to himself, interfering with that steady, pounding beat, asking permission.

The reason is that through all these imported tee shirts, art deco hair-dos, and tanned shoulders, he has recognized Laura, who gets out of a pistachio-colored Torino and heads toward an empty table. He plants himself in her way, but she does not recognize him immediately and has to ask his name. Can it be fear he sees flaring up in her eyes? As if reading his mind, she quickly hugs him but does not speak. He asks her to take him away, somewhere else, anywhere else. She squeezes his hand, smiles, nods.

She only speaks minutes later, once they have left the high-income ghetto behind, once they have reached a less noisy section of Libertador. He recognizes the scent of trees in the air.

"When did you get back?"

Just a couple of hours ago, he tells her, and he recovers the sense of unreality, a feeling that once again he will be cunningly distracted by some specific bit of information: now it is the names of streets—Serrano, Las Heras—that occasionally flash through the darkening leaves, or a lighted bar on some corner: only a few tables, but open so very late . . .

"Where'd you like to go?"

He cannot think of a place and just asks her to park, anywhere. For a moment they stand without speaking, listening to a dense silence heavy with indecipherable murmurs, their eyes following some passerby until the distance deletes him or a doorway unexpectedly whisks him away.

Not looking at him, she has begun talking in a low, unemotional voice.

"How many times I loathed you, imagining how satisfied you must be with the way things turned out . . . You never believed there could be any change, you seemed proud of remaining immune to so much promise, so much happiness, to the mere possibility . . . You looked at us skeptically, with one of those hindsight smiles you like to put on . . ."

Even while listening to her, trying to understand what impelled her to dig up all that, each word turns into an irresistible magic carpet taking off for a private Arcadia. Thus he is able to pay a return visit to some days in 1970, to images and sounds of a rescinded era, which suddenly light up as the deserted sets fill with phantasmal crowds and lines out of filed-away dialogue. Connected by very loose editing and one playback, a series of incidents pass before his eyes, sequences that, quite surprisingly, seem less glorious to him than to the actors who perform them—even though he may be one among them, even though over the years he has often recalled some fragile happiness associated with the period. Thus, like the preview of a bygone coming attraction, in already faded De Luxe color, he dusts off nights out dancing with friends—less turned on by grass than by the Jefferson Airplane (or was it Iron Butterfly? or Tangerine Dream?): he, incapable as a teenager of following the prescribed steps for dancing in couples, would only, well into his twenties, let himself learn from the '60s that movements could be invented, suggested by the music, watching whoever dances in front of you, or in front of somebody else, open to being a pair or a group or staying alone, and later going home, to somebody's house, since it was not always the same person, and making love, maybe, or just listening to Janis, or both, falling asleep (one hour? two?) before an alarm clock goes off at five and Laura picks out her most anonymous clothes, improvises an instant coffee with hot water from the tap, and grabs a cab that will cost a fortune to take her to some factory on the outskirts of town, where she will arrive just in time to hand out her Trotskyite pamphlets to the morning shift, before going back home and immediately resuming her interrupted sleep.

She was still sound asleep hours after he got up, took a shower, shaved, dressed, got breakfast without trying to be quiet, even emphasizing the noises, before leaving for the publishing house where a job waited, something he did not have to worry about, knowing it was temporary, because he was keeping himself available (even then!) for those bigger and better things he knew life held in store for him. She would call him in the afternoon to find out where they would eat; if he had not received passes for some premiere, perhaps to remind him about a party it would be criminal not to attend.

How long did it last? Weeks? Months? A year? Now it comes back, all of it, with the sharp focus of a single night, and, at the same time, with a huge cast of characters and events, as though it had lasted who knows how long . . . Recalled now, how flimsy it all seemed! Stained glass over tin, wreaths of paper flowers between bare walls, without the stereophonic effects that could transform such banal reality into true fiction . . . Once again ashamed of contaminating his feelings with literary reminiscences (James and "the real thing," Auden on the emotive power of popular music), he tries to concentrate on this present Laura at his side, on the unemphatic voice, whose words try to wound him and might succeed if they were not directed at some distant stand-in for himself.

"What obscene satisfaction you must have taken in your own misgivings when time proved you right . . ."

How to tell her that what she calls "the way things turned out" brought him no personal satisfaction, although the fall of some self-elected gray eminence might have pleased him? But this is not the moment to recall that for some months her friends at the university had imposed the study of Eva Perón's apocryphal prose as literature, that the marriage of the words "national" and "popular" had given birth to endless pompous cultural abortions. He chooses to ask her how she managed during "the transition."

"Papa was able to clear my record. You know, he's with the economic mission in Washington . . . He also paid to clean up my younger brother's, who was strutting around with armed groups in Rome and Madrid: even he, dumb as he is, ended up realizing there was nothing left to do, and now he's back. And he's making out quite splendidly . . ."

After a moment of silence she adds: "So, you've come back to spy on us . . ."

Would she understand if he confessed that far from spying he is dazzled by this sunken Atlantis, rising miraculously out of the nocturnal ocean, conjured up by some unsolicited wave of a magic wand? How much longer will these streets, which usually aroused no more than his daytime impatience, offer themselves up to nostalgia? He cannot detect any greenish trace of moss on the facades (are there buildings behind?), no glimpse of unconvincing sleepwalking among the extras. If he wanted to—he tells himself—he could touch them. But could he really? Would he dare reach out? And even if he did, what would that prove? That he is more real than they? Maybe some unknown power has granted him this single night, and it will not be the others who vanish at dawn, when the light of day regains its authority.

He gets up his courage to ask her something: Does she know if Enrique's still alive?

"Enrique?"

When he says the family name, she reacts brusquely.

"How should I know?"

He tells her that, of course, he knows all about it: how they beat him, taking him from his house in the middle of the night, how they tore up his apartment, the blood stains on the walls and staircase after they dragged him down five flights to the blue car, without plates, waiting in the street. But, isn't there some chance he's still alive?

When she answers, she speaks very slowly, as if spelling new words to a dull student.

"If you don't know . . . Maybe he's not there. Maybe he's not in Paris but in Madrid, or Barcelona. Most likely Barcelona, right?"

Now, putting on a smile, she bares her teeth.

"Isn't Barcelona a center of gay life?"

The Cheshire smile still hangs shining in the air after the words have gone out.

She has started the car once again. Now they are going down Corrientes toward the obelisk: theaters, cafés, bookstores throb with nomadic nighttime crowds. He might think these postcards had been exhumed from his own memory's collection, if her voice, starting up again, did not color them with the sharp hues of the present.

"The difference between us is that I've always been, and still am, part of something. You, on the other hand . . . you always were a spectator, you kept yourself apart, without participating. Then as now. I never had so much fun as when I went with hundreds of others to beat the drum for the Old Man's return. I don't deny it: we filled the streets, we almost pulled down the trees with so many people perched up in the branches. And we roared when he came out on the balcony and waved to us! Now then, if it's real life we're going to talk about, I've learned a bit. I'm part of it now. I earn enough in public relations, the World Soccer Championship brought in enough for me to buy the apartment where I live, and my steady job pays for a lot more than three visits to the analyst each week. And by the way: even the analysts have learned something; these days you won't hear them talking about the dissolution of the ego, of taking off straitjackets, and listening to the voice from the wonderful world of schizophrenia. Remember all that crap? These days Rastochi gets $200 an hour, but he guarantees that in three months you will be capable of earning money."

Sleeping Beauty has not only awakened: she has also spoken. She has said what she feels, and the price he must pay for having dared to kiss her is to watch her shrivel, dry up, turn into a sententious witch.

They have parked beneath the word Restaurant in neon letters. The sign looks familiar. Suddenly, he recognizes it: the old Edelweiss . . . Somebody comes out, the doors part for an instant, and he catches a glimpse of the fake Bavarian decor that used to amuse him so, the damp-stained prints of views of the Starnbergersee. He thinks he's getting a silent signal from Laura, and he tells her how moved he is that she has remembered the place where they had so many dates. She laughs—a hollow, shrill laugh, like a worn-out 78 record.

"You think I remember? You think anybody remembers anything? What you recall doesn't matter to anybody. If I let you talk, you're capable of mentioning Pasaje Seaver . . . If anybody remembers it, it's to give a sigh of relief it doesn't exist anymore. Tortoni's, on the other hand, is still on Avenida de Mayo. Why don't you pay it a visit and play at recapturing what never was yours in the first place? Get it straight: they're gutting the city for highways, they're pulling down blocks and blocks of houses, whole neighborhoods. When they save an old house, it's to restore it and convert it into some chic restaurant. Did it seem like a noisy city to you? When they finish, all you'll be able to hear is cars, and you'll scarcely be able to breathe on the street. They used to say it imitated Paris? Look, now it's not even imitating Los Angeles: it's imitating Caracas, Mexico City. It was an ugly city and it's not going to be any less ugly, but in the process a lot of people are going to earn a lot of money. So get it into your head: I don't remember. *You* remember—if you want to. Now, please, get out."

Once again more responsive to the set than to the actors, he gets out of the car without so much as a farewell glance for this creature capable of rejecting her own image in another's memory. He stops still at the entrance. Does he dare cross the threshold? What would happen if he met the usual people? Maybe there was an opera tonight at the Colón and some of the audience is having a late-night supper: they remark whether Oswald has added to his collection of garden dwarfs and cuckoo clocks, and Erico's reedy voice still cuts in to put an end to all possible discussion: "But you should have heard Jeritza . . ."

The doors open again and out of a '30s movie comes the old flower seller, already a nostalgia icon in the '60s: now as then she has dyed yellow hair, full of hairpins that flatten lifeless curls against her temples, and her basket overflowing with nosegays of violets mixed in with jasmine. (At one time he knew her name: a dubious literary impulse led him to ask her to have a glass of wine with him now and again, to make up for his never buying her flowers.) The old woman looks at him and smiles faintly. He returns the smile. Can she have recognized him? For a second she stands motionless, a curious, almost ironic twinkle in her eyes. Then she slowly moves away.

He does not go in. Neither does he go away. Although the traffic noises get no quieter, they seem to doodle a hypnotic, goading murmur, and he feels the danger of staying there, wrapped in his own bewilderment.

A voice breaks the spell. Someone has called his name. He turns. They call again and only then, behind the wheel of a car stopped in the middle of the street, does he recognize Felipeli, who waves a hand and smiles spiritedly. Is it possible he hasn't changed either? He looks the same as years ago, perhaps too identical: his exaggerated features summed up in the broad strokes of a caricature.

Felipeli unfurls an arrogant friendliness, which reminds him of the ambiguous camaraderie of military service, the petty executioner lurking inside the loud-mouth buddy. Felipeli says he is so happy to see him, pats him on the ribs, scrapes a cheek lightly against his, announces that he wants to take him for a drink. In point of fact, he is much shorter than he . . . why does he find this effusiveness threatening? He observes the hands that grasp the wheel: those nails are still the same shiny shells, manicured for years . . . When Felipeli used to push a bountiful cart with hot coffee, soft drinks, and packaged pastries, he already wore that same conciliatory, resilient smile. He went from floor to floor of the office building where the publishing house had its offices, offering the chance to take a coffee break in the various magazines' news rooms; he never stopped smiling, not even when he knew everybody knew, unquestionably, that he reported to the army's intelligence service (what was that branch of the political police called?) floating phrases, one side of telephone conversations, passing remarks, bits and pieces picked up during his affable alimentary rounds.

Felipeli, who perhaps has never heard of Unamuno, has devoted his life to contradicting him with spontaneous zeal: he has always been, and undoubtedly always will be, on the winning side. An old-time complicity inherited from his early career with the police—a tie he prefers to call "the buddy spirit"—freed him from what he now calls "journalistic slavery" and let him move, in the entourage of a minister, in high Libyan circles: "Here I am," he points out on a prematurely faded Polaroid, "when we signed the oil contracts." His friend and protector left the country without warning, leaving an hysterical lady president as hostage: the same powers who worked to bring them down granted him leave to go, when he agreed to keep quiet about so many army officials' deals with that regime. But Felipeli was ready now for his own *cursus honorem*: at the moment of stepping up the fight against subversion, men with his experience became invaluable. Now he hears him quote, with brazenness sanctioned by familiarity, a certain naval school, a certain detention camp, which have become synonyms for horror. "Want me to tell you something? Pleasant, what's *called* pleasant, it wasn't. But if it was necessary to start all over again, I'd be there—that's where you learn what a human being is."

Is Felipeli aware of his misgivings about naturalism? In any case, he spares him the catalogue of the electric prod, the iron bar, shot off fingers, drugged bodies dumped from airplanes at night. Instead, he chooses to praise military virtues tempered by the challenge of war ("a war, sure; maybe even a dirty war to boot, but a necessary war"), to evoke the solidarity pledged forever with a weapon passed from hand to hand, since spilled blood seals a mystic brotherhood of executioners, or the circle of uniforms around a table on which lay a manacled body, bludgeoned by each one, so there is no crusader left who has not paid the price of his glory. It does not surprise him that so much euphemistic jargon turns up again in Felipeli's emotion-filled voice ("transfer" for unrecorded executions, "boating" for the car ride a prisoner was forced to take, during which he was supposed to point out any passerby he had ever associated with in "subversion"), words from which he has shielded the language in which he learned to write.

Less explicit connections begin to show up as well, ones he had intuited and Felipeli now illuminates with unrelenting precision, perhaps because he sees them as less obscene than mere physical pain. He thus discloses the undisguised admiration of career bureaucrats in the army, accustomed to coups d'etat carried out by telephone and to seats on the local boards of directors of international companies, for impatient amateurs eager to take all the risks, to prove themselves in feats of arms whose audacity those same officials could never imitate because they were planned and conducted clandestinely; but also the victim's insidious respect for his executioner, that adversary capable of subduing him, subjecting him, and, above all, of knowing how to hold on to power; since, after all, it is a question of power, and, for some reason, those who anoint themselves with the most romantic attributes of rebellion get off on imitating the military organization with its system of rank, uniforms, discipline; and between executioner and victim, more eloquent than the banal erotic pact, an understanding is established: between So-and-so and So-and-so, yesterday pals at the Brothers' school, today enemies who find themselves on the same plane between Rome and Madrid—one travelling on an official mission, with a rank and uniform befitting that credible convention called real life, the other with cash for an armed group that in exile perpetuates a pure fiction of uniforms and ranks—and they cannot help hugging and then laughing at the roles life has cast them in; of the lower-middle-class official having to apply electricity to a militant whose name epitomizes the upper class, and bridging the intermissions, those pauses so essential for the body to regain feeling, by asking him how he dresses for the racetrack, what restaurants are suitable for asking his girlfriend out to dinner, if Saint-Tropez is still fashionable. Felipeli laughs, as if admitting that his stories only perpetuate the coarse folklore of military service: "Believe it or not, lots among them had streets named after their families . . . They were spared: not all of them, but enough; from the poor devils, a lot fewer; from the kikes, none."

The car does not stop. Now they are passing through neighborhoods he does not recall, maybe never saw before, his acquaintance with this city he continues to call his own being so spotty: streets silent and dark, windows stubbornly shut, a scene that promises neither peace nor literature, and only seems to be on the look-out, controlled, spiteful, as during a truce. It is a setting for Felipeli's voice, relentlessly surveying it, never stopping, populating it with an incessant, apparently self-generating narrative.

What is he telling now? Nothing he does not already know: about sociologists and psychiatrists freed from interrogation to join the repression, contributing varied backgrounds and technical skills, all useful; about a very beautiful prisoner who volunteered to infiltrate a group of mothers of *desaparecidos* and handed over a few so as to take revenge on her mother-in-law, far removed from any kind of militancy but polished off with accusations as false as they were convincing and sent to a quick, final disappearance; about exiles who agreed to censor their testimony to international organizations so as to respect the political line of their group, and also about those who answered the call of a travelling admiral, busy inventing an illusory political future for himself, and agreed to talks on neutral territory, fancying a no less illusory political future for themselves. Shrewd stage manager, Felipeli does not forget the need for comic relief: the girl prisoner snatched from torture to become part of that same official's entourage and eventually finger her ex-accomplices, the presumed organizers of an attack during the trip, compels the soldiers guarding her to run out at ten at night to buy her an evening dress at the L'Etoile drugstore, since—as she explains—she would embarrass them at Maxim's in the same clothes she wore from the prison cell to the plane.

Felipeli's laughter is frank, enthusiastic. In it he recognizes something deeply authentic, which he does not know how to fight, or has learned it is useless to fight, since it brings together murderers and the murdered, irrevocably expelling those who do not know how to laugh along with them.

After a while he does not listen any more.

They have returned to the center of town, and he would rather watch the people walking on the streets. He recalls that tireless coming and going, that sleepwalking, from his first times out on the street all night as an adolescent: breathing in deeply, eyes wide open, glowing at the tacit promise of excitement everywhere, admitted into the occult yet so accessible mysteries of the night. Years later, here he is, trying again to catch the look of those passersby, trying to read from their faces who they are, where they are going.

They look tired, happy, impatient, vacant, rushed, sad: like people on the streets of any city. And they do not see him. Of course he does not forget that he is examining them from a moving car . . . but, on the other hand, why should they look at him? Doesn't he feel like a phantom himself? A shameless Rip van Winkle, trying to explain the current landscape with a tattered, yellowed Baedeker, mixing up his memories with facts, mistaking his desires for impressions . . . ?

But this is not the whole truth. Nor does he want to give up whatever he has been allowed to salvage from the past. He starts saying names: names he knows, names he remembers, names crossed out that suddenly he has decided he does not want forgotten. He knows no one listens to him, that even if they were listening, most likely they would not react, but this does not stop him from playing the part of an uninvited Tiresias, not cursed with the gift of foretelling the future but with the most devaluated of currencies: memory. He summons up cars without license plates, children abandoned on highways, countless corpses tied to stones, so many they turned riverbeds and lake bottoms into submarine cemeteries. And other names, more names. And, always, impunity for killers belonging to a single faction—the one in power.

He cannot stop. It does not matter that Laura mockingly reminds him that they were not his friends, that he could not stand many of them, that even if they were alive he would not want to see them. Guillermo does not dissuade him either by asking him to be honest and admit that all he really misses are the endless afternoons on Viamonte Street in the days when the old Facultad was there, when he would enter and leave lecture halls, cafés, bookstores in a single, directionless movement, or the slow walk back home through deceptively peaceful streets after the midnight show at the film society, or the fickle friends, and also maybe the first awkward pangs of love. He does not grow silent even when realizing that all he really wants back is his carefree, squandered, irretrievable youth.

Now they are all in the car, crowded around him, smiling, tugging at his sleeve in a friendly way, clapping him on the back. They go through a park (can it possibly be Parque Centenario?) and the sounds of the city reach them muffled by the trees and the distance. At regular intervals, the light from solitary lampposts lets him make out in their faces expensively capped teeth, impeccable cosmetic surgery, almost invisible lobotomy scars. They never stop smiling. They produce a shiny rectangle of plastic, a boarding pass, and their voices merge in familiar, perhaps spontaneous polyphony:

"Did you think we didn't love you anymore?"

"Because you forgot us, we were going to forget you?"

"Come on, join us. This pass lets you on."

"Act like a man, give up that painted cardboard limbo, take the plunge into reality."

"Aren't you tired of being a tourist? Haven't you seen enough cathedrals, palaces, and museums?"

"Nothing gathers moss here."

"You've got a place with us, *your* place."

"Give us your ticket, and we'll give you the boarding pass."

"You know we're the best, always were, they can't have brainwashed you that much . . ."

"Let's see . . . Give us your ticket . . . Come!"

Then he confesses that he does not have it. He tries to explain that it was no longer valid, that he burned it a few hours ago.

"You burned it? What are you saying?"

"Come off it, quit joking."

"We're not going to believe just anything that pops into your head, just because you haven't any luggage with you."

"You really burned it?"

"You went crazy?"

"Let's see! Make it come back."

"You make movies, don't you?"

"It's an easy trick, they do it in the movies all the time, must be second nature for you . . ."

Suddenly he begins to wish along with them. If only he could, in reverse motion, make the charred paper rise from the ashes, and on the paper a ring of flames, a palpitating firey little rose that would slowly burn out to leave in its place, intact, the last page of his ticket . . .

Why not? After all, history is endlessly rewritten. Maybe it only exists to be rewritten? They do it by paying for twelve pages in the *New York Times* and six in *France Soir*, explaining "the question of human rights" in the middle of advertisements for international hotels, import groups, and new branches of the Banco de la Nación. Why shouldn't he want to recover his ticket?

But he cannot find any ashes. From his pocket he produces only the key to the apartment on Uriburu Street where he lived for almost thirty years. They are not impressed.

"What's the sense, keeping that key?"

"Is it a fetish?"

"Rubbish! After all, you're not a Jew from Toledo."

Then he realizes that if they can hurt him it is because they know him well. They remember that he never played at terror, neither dressing up as a gaucho bandit nor squeezing a little red book in his fist. They know he left when the Old Clown was still alive, and they also have to know that, when it comes to trained monkeys, he does not see a big difference between the Zombie Widow with her travelling-circus Cagliostro and the interchangeable starched uniforms playing Monopoly with rival intelligence services.

They go on laughing, but now they have begun to hit him.

"Burning your return ticket! So that's how much your friends mean to you!"

"You aren't one of us anymore."

He covers his head to shield himself from the blows, and gathering all his strength, lunges for the door, groping for a handle he cannot see.

Now he is running across the damp lawn and the fading shouts reach his ears in isolated blasts.

"We'll turn your books into best sellers!"

"A million people will go to see your movies!"

"Here you'll have the place you deserve!"

"This is *your* place!"

It gets darker every minute, every minute colder. One after another the lights go out and he cannot make out the lines of elms and China trees, he can only feel his agitation while listening to the faint rustling of the leaves in the breeze. Is he really in Parque Lezama? Or has he lost his way among the slopes and intermittent lakes of Parc Montsouris? Will Parque Patricios leave him stranded in the middle of Parc Monceau? He reaches a hand out into the darkness and his fingers burn as if he had unexpectedly touched ice. What is this tombstone doing here? No, the Recoleta cemetery is not Père Lachaise and he will not yield to a terminal case of bad translation.

His heart beats as fast as if he were running for his life. He stops and hears his breathing as if it were not his, as if he had detected an ominous whisper in the woods. Fast! Fast! Before everything is obliterated! Before he too is obliterated?

He shuts his eyes and cannot tell whether it is because he is afraid of seeing the last of Buenos Aires vanish or because he is afraid of listening, once again, to its siren song.

(1978-1980)

THE POSTCARD ALBUM OF THE JOURNEY

The city where I was born and raised. The city where everything happened. I ran away, but you can't run away from the landscape of your dreams. My nightmares are still set in the streets of . . .

Ross Macdonald, *The Chill*

(Early Nothing)

Children ecstatically watching a slide show will, after a moment, come to notice the texture, however polished, of the screen where fleeting visions of pagodas, fjords, and bedouins alight. Their fascination with such transient wonders will not be impaired by an acknowledgement of the silvery fabric allowing mere light to be reflected in ever-changing colors and shapes. It matters little if, instead of the woven or synthetic texture of a screen, that surface is a grainy or slick wall—accidents of paint or paper only bring out dramatically the nature of the support. Recognition of blinding or dim intervals between slides amounts to a welcome fall from grace, to a thrilled admission into the realm of knowledge.

We were born in a city called Buenos Aires and lived there for many years. The city is, legally, a federal district and the capital of Argentina, a republic on the southern corner of South America, as endemically prone to living beneath its means as its capital is to living above hers. The overgrowth of that mercantile harbor city, its impatience with the motley collection of territories gathered into a country she would nevertheless pay little attention to, its sensitiveness to imported fads, to the prestige of mere distance—all these facts have earned lip-service from worried men of letters and hit-and-run politicians alike.

Now that we no longer have to bear with the city's alternating fits of despondency and self-assertion, when we think of her we realize that, if a divorce really exists between capital and country, then we are the children of Buenos Aires, not of Argentina. For it is chlorinated tap water, random urbanism, and fast city talk that made us—not the empty immensity of the pampas, neither crystal-clear mountain lakes nor drowsy jungles.

For almost a century and three quarters, a variety of social and political fictions have been projected, like so many slides, on the Argentine screen—enlightened despotism, folkish bloodshed, liberal democracy, populist and military depredation. The only thing they had in common was the brittle nature of an optical illusion. City streets and whole provinces changed names but their dwellers did not give up their skepticism. Constitutions, launched or annulled, were variably ignored. Some people got rich, some people got killed. The less ingrained the convictions, the more vehemently a new government would invoke traditions, a style of life, ethos, and religion: people would take a minute off from their fretful somnambulism to nod their approval before going back to minding their own business.

The intervals between these historical slides were seldom noticed. Unlike sudden cracks in a labored make-up, they would not expose ghastly wrinkles or jaded skin, but that most damnable, unacceptable fact—mere absence, light on a blank surface. When we noticed this, we did not feel allowed into a joyful knowledge, though it may have proved to be a liberating one, when not stunning. It made us aware: we had been taking a fiction for reality, and even those among us most doggedly dedicated to living up to their dreams resented being cast in an unsolicited play.

Thus, hastily or with deceptive leisure, colorful romances and realistic dramas, chorus lines and *kammerspiel* visited the screen, all to vanish, leaving behind a sense of phantasmagoric intricacy and a resilient taste of nothingness. History is nobody's business, the invisible prompter would whisper, and, indeed, impermanence seemed to be its only enduring attribute. In the end vegetative indifference preserves the living vegetables; monsters thrive on monstrosity, and dreams kill the dreamers.

A country where history, far from being rewritten, is diligently removed, sealed, mummified, may end up as a country without any history at all. Where resolution is avoided, the past is denied the breathing space of historical life. Its conflicts and characters linger on, hovering about with the bland persistence of serviceable zombies. One person's bogeyman, another's savior, lives forever. A hundred years after his death, the name of Rosas is vindicated or vituperated in ubiquitous graffiti; a hundred years after his death, the name of Perón may haunt the unforeseeable walls of future architectures.

For the once quiescent infants in Plato's cave, there may be no end to the moving shadows on the wall. Those living closer to the entrance are, inevitably, the first to become curious about the real world outside. But their minds will fashion it after the desires aroused by those same shadows. Films are the obvious, voluble go-between of this suspended knowledge. Shreds and bits of reality lend consistency to their fiction, and among cave dwellers those who develop an appetite for outer space always find in them renewed food for longing.

Then, one day, we wandered away from the cave. The realm of originals, like Vermeers too often reproduced on the lids of butter-cookie boxes, struck us with simultaneous shocks of recognition and disillusion. We did not feel in their presence the pregnancy and urgency that, we were told, are the hallmark of existential revelation. Nor did we become instant performers, our surroundings the pliable decor for a long-awaited audition. At home, the luminous cave walls had always receded at the touch of eager fingertips; now, the too solid volumes of the outside world, no longer figments of light and shadow, add up to a vast, indifferent museum, waiting to be scrutinized on a conducted tour. Is it too late to achieve the metamorphosis from enforced spectator into regular actor?

Once in the open, we find the air less heady than dry. In retrospect, the years of vicarious life and apprehensive expectations start to look like a dress rehearsal for an opening night that may be cancelled. Or the landscape, wearing thin after a first inspection, starts to look like a second (magnified, boundless) cave. Furthermore—doesn't everything remind us, less of its reproduced, debased image, than of the impending catastrophe that was to smash that image?

We look back and Argentina appears to us like a choice arena where the larger bankruptcy of steadier societies was enacted earlier and more brutally. Down there, proprieties of aped culture and borrowed notions of justice and decorum gave way more easily. While the metropolis welcomes, accomodates, seduces, and tames barbarians, peripheral countries are simply run over by them.

To enjoy the tour we need to ignore the writing on the wall reminding us of a distant prophetic doom. Or else forget what the movies promised and discover a nameless pleasure in the oil tower at the fjord's entrance, in the Rolls the bedouin is driving, in the dazibao pasted on the pagoda wall.

To each his own barbarians.

(1977)

What shall we do without barbarians?
These people were some sort of solution . . .

C. P. Cavafy, "Waiting for the Barbarians"

Civilization comes near its end when even barbarians flee from
it.

Karl Kraus, *Aphorisms*

Fascist Lullaby

Heads slicked down with brilliantine into art deco, metallized, glossy cannon balls, a hint of sticky permeability in its sweet vegetal fragrance . . .

Perhaps . . . But it sounds a little abstract . . .

Cider and Christmas pudding, Christmas pudding and cider, and on October 17 the smell of pork sausages on street-side charcoal grills near the Plaza de Mayo . . .

It is already more concrete, but a little trivial.

The German tightrope walkers coming and going on iron threads stretched between the tip of the obelisk and the dome of the Trust Joyero Relojero . . .

Too private. Does anybody else remember them?

Tibor Gordon, healer and preacher, gathering thousands under his suburban circus tent, while a shocked, incredulous Catholic church watched the regime it had helped enthrone suddenly, unaccountably, turning against it . . .

Could do. But why not something less exceptional? Those "tango streets," perhaps?

He would walk her back home. Once there, the home-grown variety of petting and necking, the natural extension of kisses and caresses would take place in the darkened hallway. In those immigrated lands such forms of intercourse had been named after a particularly soft cloth. *(Even today, writing in another language, so far away, so much later, do you remember the obscenity that word conveyed?)* Yes. Flannel . . .

One ear listening for the family asleep in the house, the other for footsteps coming this way in the street, they stayed there half an hour, no, an hour.

But would not Father be aware of the shapes across the crotcheted curtain of the second front door, on his way to and from the toilet in the middle of the night? Would not Mother follow the unmistakable sighing and panting with suspended unease or vicarious apprehension? Would not Kid Brother peep at those telling, larger-than-life shadows, his naked feet on the patio tiles, his eager prepubescent penis clasped in fraternal anticipation?

He used to come in his underpants. She would feel, with mixed regret and relief, the diminishing pressure on her stomach. "One more night and always a virgin, one step closer to marriage." She would still think it weeks later, when he opened his fly and muttered into her ear, "Please, please," in an unexpected childish tone, while taking her hand and filling it with the stiff, warm, throbbing object. She would hesitate between shaking it, just to be released sooner, or clumsily fondling it to display her inexperience. But her mind was really on the new dress, the flimsy summer fabric, the delicate print she would preserve from that sticky horror.

He would not come again in his underpants, sticky cold when riding the bus back home, smelly sticky later the same evening while undressing in his boarding-house room before yielding to the austere familiarity of mended bedsheets.

No, he would not. His chin on her shoulder, he would let himself go and feel how her hand, directing the shot sideways, only increased the final flash of elation. His hair would be shaken, greasy brilliantine would shed a dry powder not unlike dandruff, reeling as the metal of the cannon ball would never do in the moment of detonation—even if sent into space, in flames, toward destruction.

(1978)

The chronicler who presents events without distinction between great and small takes into account this truth: nothing that ever happened should be lost for History. . . . The real image of the past rushes away. The past may only be grasped as an image that, in the moment it is recognized as such, shines for the last time.

Walter Benjamin, "Thesis on the Philosophy of History"

(Star Quality)

Yesterday night I dreamt of her. She was on TV, all gray and bluish, and didn't seem to like it. She wanted to get back into radio, and I promised her I would help. The absence of feedback left her looking distressed and me with a sour taste of impotence. When I woke up this morning I knew I would never make a film about her. I had toyed with the idea for years. I had written down sequences of it. I had seen definite images in my mind—I remember how they were lit, where a cut linked and separated them.

I may be a coward for not trying. What am I afraid of? That my mixed, fascinated feelings for her might clash with the hagiography demanded by her forlorn fans? That they might insult me? That they might even try to harm me? Or is it really that I am afraid of becoming, in the process, one of them?

I can recall the never-to-be opening shot of thick fog at sunrise, being slowly pierced by an indefinite, approaching dark shape that becomes an old woman driving an open cart across the pampas. She is an Indian midwife. Some hours earlier she has received word that the delivery would not take long. She is conveniently wrinkled and inscrutable.

How appropriate that it should have been one of the last of a race bound to extinction who helped her into life. Also—that her origins, as befit the hero or the saint, should have been obscure and obscured, not least by herself as an adult. The page where her birth was noted down would be torn out of the village register when she became notorious and powerful. How could she be sensitive to those petit-bourgeois strictures that made her, a bastard, persona non grata? For those who hated her she was already the whore, as every woman who reaches beyond the role society assigns her always is.

That society could not tolerate any mixture of genres nor any fantasy in casting. Its ideas of farce and melodrama were sharply defined, and there was no middle ground. When her father died, her mother put all four children in a sulky and drove them to the wake. Recognized for years as the once-powerful local caudillo's "second family" (the three girls and the boy all bore his name), they were nevertheless denied entry by the "legitimate" widow. Only when the priest (such a colorful, unabashed Latin soap-opera contrivance!) brought both widows' hands together, surely unaware that he was re-enacting Brigitte Helm's gesture between Capital and Work at the end of Thea von Harbou's *Metropolis*, did the two women tearfully embrace, surrounded by the gaping progeny of the prolific dead man. Really, only the more formalized Mexican tearjerkers can, for those interested in the aesthetic fallacy of reflection, tell about an agrarian society nurtured on imported Spanish Catholicism . . .

The mother entertained travelling salesmen in their home-turned-boarding-house. One sister got a low-paying job at the local post-office, but even for that political influences had to be secured. The brother left for the big city. Movies were already talking by then, but there was no cinema in the village. Every evening, people would gather around a radio set. Some were square boxes with rounded tops, others were fancier, cathedral-shaped structures of wood-work and grainy cloth. Oddly moaning or screeching melodies from the hit-parade, news delivered by announcers moved by the simultaneity itself they were achieving, the intricate plots of novels in installments with declamatory overtures and mini-climaxes under-scored by much brass and fiddle, the rib-nudging jokers, the nameless voices on the commercials . . . these odds and ends produced something different but coincident: a world elsewhere, and the absence of (a then unthinkable) image endowed it with a generous capacity to welcome any plot its isolated listeners cared to weave around it.

I like to think of her, described by everybody as a moody girl with few friends, not at all keen on prowling suitors, absorbed in those sounds from outer space. She would never be a film star, though they tried to make her one, and on stage she barely went beyond "Dinner is served" or "The horses are ready," according to period and milieu. She knew, though, minute hopes and humiliations. She had to wait for hours to get to see a minor editor who might find a place for her photograph on page 64 of *Sintonia*. One opening night a bunch of yellow roses was misplaced in her hand by an inexperienced back-stage assistant who didn't realize the leading lady of the company had the same first name she did; later, the diva, who catered to those same upper-middle-class audiences who would feel most offended by her a few years later, went to the dressing room shared by six minor players in order to retrieve the bouquet, and there uttered words one of them would remember once in power.

Actually, I think she remembered everything: mainly those selves she left behind as she proceeded to add new roles to the only career that, after a certain moment (which?), she must have known was the only one that really mattered. Thus, radio was the medium through which, every night at eight, she could reach the people who had looked down on her, back home, and tell them, "Here I am"; just as power was the instrument that, some years later, allowed her to answer that diva whose ill-advised line had stayed on her mind. It was radio that allowed her to play Catherine the Great, Florence Nightingale, and Madame Chiang Kai-shek in that prophetic series that must have provided her with a basic libretto for the situations she would soon face outside the sound stages.

Nevertheless, there must have been a day, an evening most probably, when nothing particular happened during the broadcast, but anyway a swift, unaccountable crack in the routine, blinding her with its unexpected radiance, must have revealed that she had no talent as an actress. Or that her talent was for other roles. Or, rather, for another stage. And the role she could perform on that other stage was one she had to create from scratch, a role that the society she lived in would not allow a woman to play. She chose, or perhaps she just meekly accepted without even realizing it, that from that moment on her life would be an outrage to some, a blessing for others. And in that society she needed, at least in the first stage, a man in order to establish her own role.

This chronology may be wrong or just uncertain. But, then, documents are sparse, untrustworthy, tainted by devotion or spite. I choose to believe that it was on that same evening when, instead of going back to her shared boarding-house room, to wash some stockings or mend a petticoat (the window half-open to let in a bit of the hopefully fresher evening air, not wide enough to disclose her busy image to the curiosity of neighbors or to the vacant attention of passersby), she let another small-time actress working at the same station talk her into coming along to a benefit—perhaps the one staged for the victims of the San Juan earthquake. A car would take them there. The friend would know "people in high places." A black sedan would open its back door. The friend's friend would grin: "So I see you brought a friend." Introductions would be exchanged. The other man in the car would extend a confident hand: "Pleased to meet you, Miss," and she would reciprocate: "The pleasure is all mine, Colonel." (Only later would she notice the pockmarks on the putrid skin, the sticker smile.)

Would she have known, at that moment?

The film, in any case, ended (will never end) there and then. That is, with her on the threshold of History. A blackout would have followed such immaculate good manners, and over a measure of black leader the traditional three blows would have sounded, raising the curtain, leading her out of the darkness, a thin line of light growing all the time broader, dazzling, deafening her, the thousands gathered under the balcony covering all of Plaza de Mayo, hailing her as she came out to them, perhaps a tiny figure in the distance for those perched on trees at the start of the Avenida de Mayo, but all the same reaching them, jolting them, making them silent and attentive and exultant and possessed by turns, with that immensely eloquent voice that loudspeakers would deform but not impair, one trained to take in its stride the primitive radio sets that would tune her in at a small village at the end of the pampas, a voice that perhaps, even at that moment of stardom, would be addressing just them.

She died a few months after television arrived in Argentina.[1]

[1]Eva Perón, "Evita," *née* María Eva Duarte, 1919, in Los Toldos, Province of Buenos Aires, Argentina. Actress of stage, screen and radio, married 1945 to Colonel Juan Domingo Perón, Secretary of Labor, to be elected President of the Republic next year. Died 1952, of cancer, in Buenos Aires.

But the people of Alexandria, a various mixture of nations, united the vanity and inconstancy of the Greeks with the superstition and obstinacy of the Egyptians. The most trifiling occasion, a transient scarcity of flesh or lentils, the neglect of an accustomed salutation, a mistake of precedency in the public baths, or even a religious dispute, were at any time sufficient to kindle a sedition among that vast multitude, whose resentments were furious and implacable.

Gibbon, *The Decline and Fall of the Roman Empire*

(Madeleine Creole)

M., an unpublished man of letters in his forties, a resigned reader of Proust and the head of the Ship Movement section in the traditional Buenos Aires daily, has stopped on his way to the paper for a quick lunch in the underground self-service on Córdoba Avenue, between Florida and San Martín.

Out of habit he first chooses a dessert, a custard topped with (synthetic) whipped cream or a (tinned) fruit salad, which shall not suffer by waiting, before standing on line at the counter for his hot course, which might grow cold were he to invert the order of his steps. As he waits he keeps an eye on the raincoat, left on the back of a chair at the chosen table, so as not to wander later, a full tray on his hands, and end up sitting next to a heavily perfumed lady or, even worse, the mother of noisy and quarrelsome children.

He has already started on the meat course when the vision of a woman at a table nearby distracts him: she does not fit into this gastronomy, into this setting. A cursory inventory, from silk stockings to straight hair held with an almost invisible tortoise-shell brooch, promises a possible character. "We may not have duchesses," he quotes himself, "but . . ."

He'd rather ignore that such a literary syndrome is responsible for so much bad literature in his own country. The distinguished passerby leaning over the narrator, the victim of a traffic accident, and muttering "God bless you" in English, shines high in the sky of snobbery not just over Argentine letters: it presumes a complaisant literary outlook on life, blurring, mitigating everyday reality with an aftertaste of unwritten fiction. In a country where the improbable becomes true more often than elsewhere, the notion of verisimilitude has tended to be narrower and punishes with unexpected severity that life called real.

To escape that obstinate grayness, the amateur of letters (rather than the writer) seeks refuge in the sublimation of an upper class he imagines more open to caprice, peopled by characters more colorful than those within his reach. An evening at the Colón Opera Theater, or just the names of its patrons printed on the program, sketch for him the great stage of the world. The family snapshot album of a great lady, produced as a coffee-table book, lulls him, casting him as a gaping waiter at the master's party.

In times of populism, that class was rebaptized "oligarchy" and made sacred as the season's villain, its myth thus confirmed to the eyes of a fiction-hungry audience. It was often retold that, around that River Plate golden age, which lasted until 1930, *belle époque* of meat and grain export, its families sailed to Europe with their own cow so the children might have fresh milk on the boat. In a period when army and union leaders headed the same way, but on planes and carrying attaché cases full of dollars destined for Swiss numbered accounts, that weathered image exhaled a certain charm.

Such sensible voyagers, did they foresee that around 1972 their great-grandchildren would devise a memorable stratagem? When a military government decided to import from exile a senile dictator, thus hoping to save their own caste and, by the way, that upper class, the greatest art collector in the country, fearing a demagogical state expropriation, quickly invited experts from Sotheby's and Christie's, whose against-the-clock estimates led to shipments toward London and Geneva of many paintings only a few dozen people had seen in the country whose work had paid for them. To the owner's astonishment, many Sisleys and Derains, even some Renoirs and a few Monets, turned out to be flagrant fakes —for some time now his grandchildren had been inviting to the family's *estancia* underpaid copyists posing as grateful art students, who during the long, tedious summers devoted themselves to duplicating the paintings less frequented by the already diminished old man . . .

"How unpleasant!" The traditional comment of this class, a transplant of British understatement, may have echoed briefly before the episode itself was buried by the robust ties of blood.

If some kind of folklore could rise around them it may be because the protection of their own interests was not always pursued in a sound manner. A lady who had secluded herself in the *estancia* during the Second World War, Paris being, for the time, off limits, ventured on one of the first, slow and stopover-prone post-war flights to Europe. Upon her return, a few months later, she dazzled friends and relatives at tea time, circulating among them her (French) Communist Party membership card: "I was strongly advised to do so. It seems they already have half of Europe and in the other half they run very influential parties. I was told that if we join among the first we shall be expropriated among the last." The same hated dictator who, by pretending to make an enemy out of them, confirmed their legend where there had only been gossip, imitated their time-honored techniques. He declared, for instance, war on the Third Reich when the Red Army was already outside Berlin, thus being able, weeks later, to appropriate the German industries in the country as "enemy property" . . . How pleasant! And his wife, whose work as a benefactor added to the fascism implicit in all displays of charity a sense of show business closer to Cinecittà than to Hollywood, was to discover unspeakable hygienic conditions at a candy factory whose owners had denied a substantial donation to her enterprise.

In this showdown of rival gangs, History bestowed alternating smiles. The greatest private fortune expropriated by the dictator was restored at the next political shakedown, with interest and in a re-evaluated currency. "Falling on your own feet" is the only moral this class has preached, by their own example. The castle on the Loire reproduced in the Province of Buenos Aires or the servants addressing dinner guests in French among the Córdoba hills have only been particles of a myth as limited as it has proven resistant.

The wayward youngsters, exported to Europe in the '20s and '30s, would around 1980 marry their granddaughters to suddenly acceptable Jewish or Italian money made on real estate or finance. Once admitted, even if only at the Country Club and not at the Jockey Club, their new family names, previously savored with giggling relish, were whisked away by a cursory delivery or plainly cancelled by turns like "So-and-so's husband."

Such wily conversationalists, were they the same who on a rainy Sunday, sometime in the '50s, with nothing much to do around the *estancia*, opened in the cellar a rusty trunk to discover, flabbergasted, *thales* and *menorah*, quickly returned to the darkness that had protected them since the distant times when the Spanish conquest brought to the country Spanish and (indistinct, unidentifiable) Sephardic names? How unpleasant!

Untouched by the Brazilian imperial folly—mirrored in a dilapidating Carnaval and inventing on a patch of razed jungle an unnecessary capital—the Argentine bourgeois epic was content with decorum in wealth, with taste in representation. What literature may their semi-gods beget? What Proust may redeem them? The writers born in their midst have ignored them in the exact measure of their talent; only feeble littérateurs have chosen to be moved by their fortunes and genealogies. The Great Lady of Letters was dead right about her own class when she quoted Sarmiento: "Aristocracy smelling of horse dung . . ." A unique character in her own country, she always had a knack for going beyond, forcing milk jam on Stravinsky or summoning a string quartet to submit Tagore, insensitive to non-Indian music, to Borodin and Debussy.

Badly in need of other people's fiction to see themselves as major characters, hazy outlines entrusted to the vicarious daydreaming of a middle class thirsty for elegance or culture (a class long incapable of accepting as fictional subjects the too familiar lies of the political business, the extravagances of sexual repression or of the no-less repressed magic, in a country where superstition is rampant) they shall endure in a washed-out imagery, guests on a banal stage—sociology's rather than literature's.

M. finishes lunch in the underground self-service on Córdoba Avenue between Florida and San Martín. He may never publish his novel, nor his diaries, nor his marginalia. Oriane and Odette have woven a flimsy, lethal web around his sensibility: too cultivated to be satisfied with film stars, too tame to plainly ignore outward signs of social prestige.

That same evening, in front of the TV set or at a film society screening, he may feel superior to a tropical number in some dusty Hollywood musical, full of incongruous palm trees and apocryphal blacks, and yet so much truer than his own, censored image of the reality he inhabits.

And now, all together, with maracas: "Down Argentine Way"!

(1980)

In any case, Petersburg is not just an illusion. It is on the maps, in the form of two concentric circles with a black dot at the center. From that mathematical point without dimension it asserts energetically its own existence. It is precisely from that point that this book's flood of words breaks loose . . .

Andrei Biely, *Petersburg*

(Shanghai Blues)

In Buenos Aires the days grow longer when you reach September. You never thought about it, why should you? Then, one evening, you happen to be in the street around seven and you notice there is still some light left in the sky. It is a very peculiar light—it wears off slowly, it leaves the dour office buildings and the high window panes, as it were, shade by shade, until a last moment comes when it stands still, a faint rose color interfering with the blue already turning to iron gray. That stillness is of course a deception. While it lasts, while you think it lasts, it seems to suffuse angry traffic and vociferous record shops with a kind of suspended magic. To what purpose? Before you can find an answer, or suspect there is none, it is gone; the sky is ink blue, the people around you have changed.

It's a die-hard delusion. Late in October, early in November, before you can get the real feeling of summer, you may be walking down Corrientes and notice the impatient housewives, loaded with shopping bags, queuing for buses, or the bank clerks, exhausted by overtime and defective air conditioning, their shirts adhering to both body and jacket in one intensity of malaise. Then the #303 bus arrives. A teenager steps out—short-sleeved shirt in full wash-and-wear splendor, head graced by haircut too expensive for the social context that comb and identity papers, detectable under the pressure of insolent buttocks, spell out from the back pockets of his jeans. And you realize what they ignore, or take for granted in unformulated acceptance—that it is shift time. Day people call it a day. Night people get ready to take over. Perhaps you also realize you are in-between—you've awakened at any hour, you've been in and out, now you may be heading for a movie or to meet a friend at some café, heedless of the well-regulated caesura that in a few hours will see the lady watching after-dinner TV, a silent husband by her side, both already changed into something more comfortable, and the boy having yet another espresso at the counter of Tazza d'Oro or Caravelle while listening to a carefully groomed gentleman, impeccably tanned even though it is so early in the season.

But it's not as easy as all that. It starts with the light, of course, but then, if you are to stick to those blocks of Corrientes that run down from Florida to Alem, so unaffectedly colorless that the city can show little else so typical of itself, there is the breeze. With one breath, it relieves the afternoon of the slowly receding heat. Though not salty (How could it be? Astonished by the breadth of the river, the discoverers called it the Sweet Sea . . .), you can smell the waterfront in the breeze, heavy with the rust of old iron, with promises of departure.

Over the years you became used to it. Walking down Viamonte, you approached a section of the city that seemed so rich in excitement: bookstores, the Facultad de Filosofía y Letras, art galleries, the Café Florida, even the odd convent with its lonesome palm tree at the corner of San Martín. What did you read in this decor of sorts? By a deceptive limelight you missed the writing on the wall, the one meant for you—a teenager, eager to read and write, to be reassured that he was not wrong, that there was no worthier adventure to be pursued.

A few months after leaving, you went back to Buenos Aires for two weeks, vaguely aware of seeing the familiar places for the last time. You ventured inside what had been the Facultad in order to get an authenticated photostat of a diploma whose original had slept for too long, among seldom-aired tablecloths, in a drawer at your mother's. The plainclothes policeman (or were they members of some paramilitary force?) searched you with expert pats along ribs and legs, while their faces wore the ingratiating smiles that movies of earlier times cast on the faces of banana-republic customs officers. (The Facultad itself had long ago moved to a less exposed section of the city; nevertheless, the government security advisors had deemed fit to call off its activities indefinitely.) As you found your way out of a brand new labyrinth of brick and mortar compartmenting what had once been a charmingly inadequate *belle-époque* cadre for academic pursuits, the old smell hit back at you. An odor that had been filed away for years, like a footnote misprinted pages away from its original asterisk. Between facades on the opposite side of Alem—brief, sudden disclosures of the painted backdrop for another play—there appeared fragments of masts, rectangles of hulls, an ill-defined assembly of signs that confronted you with your own figure, walking down those same steps, fifteen years younger, yet so much wiser, with an unspoiled gift for leisure. Time of course was already keeping its steady pace, but then you could afford to ignore the winged chariot hurrying near. Why is it that you, who have never travelled by boat, should attach to their visual or fragrant neighborhood such a Baudelairian pregnancy? Baudelairian indeed! Too used to contradictio-in-adjecto, you neglected the simple evidences of explicatio . . . (Books can only lead, like unfailing go-betweens, to the desire that preceded the reading.)

And by eight in the evening you would be sitting at a street-side table, waiting for somebody who had obviously forgotten about the appointment—or given it a realistic second thought. Yet you didn't care. The dimming brightness granted the concrete blocks an unexpected nautical grace, as if any minute now they would sail away and whisk you out of a city that so stubbornly turns its back to the water, yet so painfully depends on what the far-away shores once promised in a long-ago forgotten moment of recklessness. As the supporting characters around you changed, you felt the impending threat of having to enjoy a good book in the quiet of home.

And, later, there were the bars. You were fourteen when you produced the throatiest possible falsetto to order a Cuba Libre: a rather innocuous mixture of rum and Coca-Cola whose name, in those drowsy middle '50s, sounded uncorrupted by the political overtones that a few years later would make it the campiest choice for a drink. The lady behind the counter appraised you cursorily, and after a while handed you a glass of the brownish, syrupy drink. You turned your head to encompass the whole range of exotica you had been allowed into: by the multicolored light of the Wurlitzer, endlessly chaining one Nat King Cole tune to another, two tired-looking girls, not even heavily made-up, were exchanging tips about the current discount sales; a few men sat quietly at their tables, in suits that might well have been bought at those same sales; an occasional sailor concentrated on his beer and only seemed to come alive to ask, in broken English, for a refill or to proceed with surprising assurance to the men's room. The names themselves of such places (May Sullivan's, Helen's, Texas, First and Last) seemed unaccountably glamorous, headier than anything they had to offer: the girls, not allowed to function as plain whores, were really full-time hostesses, kept awake on massive doses of tea, which they sipped with a relish usually reserved for whiskey. Their greater talent was to postpone for uncheckable after-hours whatever other interests their customers might entertain.

(How shabby those slices of a low life that plainly existed elsewhere! If by those same hopeless '50s you hadn't read Durrell's travelogues, you'd never have expected to find here a glimpse of the fast decaying prestige of harbor life. When not naive, you would be careless. Your grandmother, the solitary link between your faithless, wholly gentilised parents and a mainly gastronomic Jewish persuasion, used to invite your family to overwhelming dinners that celebrated (what for you was) a bonus New Year. At one of those occasions, you offered by way of table-talk the ultimate blunder: to more observant cousins, back from kibbutz holidays in Israel, you remarked that the place you really cared to visit in the Near East was Alexandria. Coming only a few months after the Suez war, the remark cast a frozen spell over the table. The old lady, displaying admirable sang-froid, showed you a possible way out: "Alessandria in Italy, I suppose. . . ." How could she know about that town in Piedmont? You were to find out much later, driving between Genoa and Venice, those ports where symmetrical ships used to leave her on her way from Argentina and take her on her way to Israel. The Alessandria road sign was there, a cue line to a belated repartee.)

Late spring evenings were the most intoxicating. At that elusive time of the day when light hesitates before making a langorous exit, when night is announced, even before you can speak of a breeze, by a certain unassuming lightness in the air, you really enjoyed sitting there, absorbed in the just discovered though yearly repeated intimations of approaching summer. How engrossing to feel those barely tangible changes taking place around you, while the city staged undistinguished crowd scenes. How easy to stay there.

To watch. To feel. To stay.

(1976)

The truth is, there is no longer any linguistic space outside bourgeois ideology. Our language comes from it, returns to it, stays locked in it. The only possible riposte is neither challenge nor destruction but, simply, theft—to break up the ancient text of culture, of science, of literature, and disperse its features in unrecognizable patterns, in the same way stolen merchandise is faked.

Roland Barthes, *Sade, Fourier, Loyola*

(Glad Rags)

I found a photograph of him in his mother's chocolate boxes turned archives—a child with short-cropped, side-parted, brilliantine-tamed wavy hair that exposed oversize ears and enhanced too expressive blue eyes.

I am sure he would go to school wrapped in an immaculately white, weekly-laundered-and-starched smock. Imposed by an Argentine law of the 1880s, a victory of Liberalism that made grade school free, non-confessional, and mandatory for all, such smocks were designed to keep off (the school) stage those social differences clothes are supposed to denounce and portray. They had, neverthelesss, collar openings, which exposed a triangle of shirt and an occasional bow tie, thus entrusted with an almost emblematic capacity for definition, only matched, less blatantly (though for connoisseurs more sharply), by the silent eloquence of shoes. Companions of rougher behavior would have their smocks torn and mended, wearing them with the unconcern of battle heroes displaying their scars; but I am sure he accepted his mother's ironing and his teachers' compliments with the same joyless compliance to a respectable fate.

Night always seemed to arrive too early at that time. Were not other people going out, meeting and drinking and dancing in brightly lit places, their lips now and then adhering in close-up, their black sedans more often than not sliding by in ever-present gloss?

Night had a plot of its own. It did not continue or develop the day's characters and episodes. The windows of a middle-class apartment in Buenos Aires revealed nothing of it to the child standing barefoot between drawn curtains and darkened panes, eager to read in the occasional passerby a clue to the mysteries of that foreign country to which he was denied a visa—Night. For him it was a time for reading under the blankets, by a battery-operated flashlight, and it would bring dreams of other stages and other costumes.

Every year, shortly before Carnaval (already by then a decaying, hopelessly untropical celebration of neighborhood dances and panic-struck children clutching the hand of a pride-blinded adult), a full-page advertisement in *Billiken* would have some twenty tiny figures in full exotic regalia over a small-type description of their costumes; at one side, in stark figures, the price of such flights of fancy was realistically spelled out. From that page he cut the Hindu Prince outfit—a splendid set of brocaded materials belonging, from upturned sandals to turban festooned around an outsize gem, to the all-time Night epic. (The thousand and one invoked in the title seemed less important than the fact that in it Haroun-el-Raschid would leave his palace every evening to assume a beggar's identity, bestowed upon him by a new set of clothes and the complicity of shadows.)

I am afraid he never got the Hindu Prince outfit. His parents had little tolerance for such exotic capers: a relatively expensive set of brightly-colored materials of dubious quality, of no practical use in daily (i.e. real) life until, in a year's time, the next opportunity for wearing them would come, when they would anyway have become too small for him . . . The idea sounded like abomination to their solid, working middle-class ears, which would allow fantasy to run as far as piano lessons. And with the years, of course, he no longer cared. That unattained alternate self, together with all the other minute technicolored outfits in the ad in *Billiken*, slipped into the same disregard that did away with Carnaval on those colorless margins of the River Plate.

A few years later long pants replaced his short ones, as still was the fashion in those last years of the stuffy pre-jeans age that marked the end of his childhood. He started to choose for himself, according to strictures of budget and a general paucity of social occasions. He was soon to learn a few devious lessons—a new suit, an expensive tie make you feel better, but, oh, only for so short a time! For clothes have a tendency to illustrate set theory, or, rather, what in logic is known as material fallacies, or fallacies of presumption. What is the good of a Cerutti tie on a shirt that would not even be blue collar, or of fashionably cut jacket and trousers on nondescript moccasins that would not even be tennis shoes?

If effortless, unconspicuous compatibility is not possible, then meaningful contrast has to be the guiding principle. Unfashionable clothes, on the other hand, are unattainably expensive in capitalistic society, where the Hun-like thrust of fashion pitilessly renovates in a matter of weeks the stacks of *couture* and neighborhood supermarkets as well. Merely old clothes, on the other hand, have to be of the highest quality to respond to recognizably dated taste, to achieve a classical status instead of a chic-shabby look. And then, of course, there is the unavoidable, ultimate test—the perfect set of clothes may remain inert, dormant, like a Stradivarius in a glass case if not produced on the right stage, their shades of choice, their sheer impact defused if they do not perform up to the challenge of social intercourse.

Later, much later, in the second half of his twenties, during a lonely visit to Europe which shook him with intimations of all the people he could have been if only he had dared, an invitation to a dinner party at the Stockholm Grand Hotel, with his name unmistakably handwritten on it, confronted him one morning with the small print on its lower left corner: black tie. What followed was a nightmarish visit, in a Gogol-Nabokovian key, to a clothes rental agency on Vasagatan, where an obsequious attendant submitted to his attention his own polished fingernails and bad breath together with a variety of garments where the sheen of the lapels and that of threadbare materials was not always discernible. Later, he would remember less the glittering event than its literal dress rehearsal, punctuated by thundering trains entering or leaving the neighboring Central Station, while he confronted in twin mirrors his own duplicated impersonation of a scarecrow. Would he have felt reassured then, had he known that a few months later the real thing was to become his?

The garment itself was to be of rather good quality, his size, and the price almost reduced by half. Always an easy prey to ideological legerdemain, he felt allowed to cheat on social pressures if buying a tuxedo at a discount sale. It seemed only fair, then, that ideology should take an immediate revenge—what would have been the first possible occasion to wear it turned out to be one of those hopeful post-1968 film festivals where film producers displayed shampooed long hair on Mao jackets and not one tuxedo was allowed . . . Seven years later, when revolt was already being filed under nostalgia, he released from cellophane covers and mothballs what had become almost a fetish of unrealized promise. It proved to have been miraculously preserved. He himself, however, was not—his overweight shape would not fit the garment he had set such wild hopes upon: very much like his life, which in its day-to-day chain of minute gestures and forecasts had fallen consistently short of the cherished image he had allowed himself to entertain.

It sounded too much like a fable not to suspect that a moral would be the only dividend of such real-life narrative. A particle of conversation, absently listened to at a cocktail party, was to illuminate a vaster territory than it intended to: a lady sociologist was gushing about her intoxicating experience in Cuba, an instance of what she described as "the release from fashion." (Up to the mid-'70s, in Buenos Aires, such verbal exercises were still frequent among advertising executives and media analysts.) He dismissed it immediately, a mere predicate of its speaker. But it stuck to his memory and a few years later, while he waited at an airport lounge, it surfaced to bring back his own fable, to make him aware of other people's.

He looked around and took it all in: the woodsman garb, complete from worn-out sweater to patched jeans, of a bush-bearded Berlitz teacher; the almost archeologically restored hippie look of city office workers on their time off; the desperate shabby-genteel tidiness of an almost proletarianized lower middle class; the Stalinist asceticism of a New York socialite. With some of them, the alternate self that clothes allow to be realized worked by intensification; with others by blunt, dazzling contrast. It could be a spelling-out or a revelation. Models could be exalted or crushed by their own compulsive choices.

He watched them come and go. The same agitation presided over them all, a motley cast of characters who did not belong in the same plot, were it not for that other-induced, self-inflicted fiction that allows people to keep on going, that collective intercourse of appearances preventing the social fabric from bursting open at numberless hidden seams.

(1976)

74

From a strictly esthetic point of view, my aim was to condense, in their almost primary state, a series of events and images I refused to exploit by letting my imagination work on them. In short: the negation of a novel.

Michel Leiris, *Literature Considered as Bullfighting*

Make the inventory of everything you feel nostalgic about . . . without explaining or relating, without links, just the things you really feel nostalgic about. Another day, make the inventory of everything you feel afraid of.

Elias Canetti, *The Human Province*

(Cheap Thrills)

For weeks I had admired from the metro window the bill-boards of the Luxor-Pathe, never short of kidnapped princesses and singing magi: a swift vision soon interfered with by the iron bridges announcing the elevated Barbès-Roche-chouart station. It was only on a cold Saturday evening last December that I ventured out of the protection of the Porte Dauphine-Nation line to inspect more closely the film offerings of that notoriously Arab neighborhood. The templelike Luxor-Pathe, I learned, was only the most impressive of several theaters specializing in the subproletariat of current film industry—on one hand the waning Italian westerns, their French sound track no less improbable than the Italian or English parlance that usually goes together with Spanish or Yugoslav locations in countertyped color; on the other, the all-pervading Kung-Fu confections from Hong Kong and Taipei, gruesome fairy tales of an industrious East. As for the old-fashioned, gaudy fairy tales, I found out that more often than not they are really Indian films, their original Bengalese or Pakistani soundtracks replaced by Arab voices that have made them favorite entertainments from Baalbek to Clignancourt.

I have forgotten which one of those sturdy-looking buildings, so alien to the diminutive chic of Left Bank cinemas *d'art et d'essai*, was showing an Egyptian vehicle for both Farid El Atrache and Chadia, singing idols of the Arab world. I can only remember my almost immediate disappointment at the lack of color and the plainly realistic locations—though a musical all right, this was not a Thousand-and-One-Nightish spectacular. The film, it turned out, was really a tear-jerker cum comedy. Its actions took place in and around an army camp, where *he* was a sergeant doomed to early death by an unspecified illness, and *she* the nurse who pierced his mistrust and understandable sulkiness, bringing some enjoyment of life to his last weeks.

My disinterest, though, gave way almost imperceptibly to a curiosity of a different kind. Every predictable bit of action looked perfectly geared, the dosage of sentiment and farce carried on smoothly as if the best, irretrievable Hollywood examples had come back to an alien, rougher life. That middle-aged ham and name-dropper who vaunts an obviously inexistent artistic career and ends up as a female impersonator, his line-thin moustache duly powdered, in the camp show; that fat, bald-headed, clumsy buddy with stomach trouble; that deaf-and-dumb sweet-looking younger soldier who paints; all of them entered and left the frame like musical instruments, alternating and combining their diverse registers to develop new harmonic variatons.

If all this looked faintly familiar, I thought, it was because it reminded me of American comedies of the Second World War, even of their uncertain post-data—the Korean war. National loyalty was obviously taken for granted, and the simple sorrows and solidary joys of barrack life were undisturbed by the complaisant self-questioning that, even before Vietnam, had crept in to stay as a new, "critical" key for Hollywood products. Near the end, when Farid El Atrache and Chadia came together on a patriotic number, an open-air parade where soldiers deftly maneuver colored panels in order to compose gigantic flags of several Arab states, I began to be moved by an emotion less visible, more devious than the one shared by the rest of the audience.

How long was it since I had watched such wholesome capers with straight attention, without a self-preserving, displaced smile? If I could share an emotion, even for such a brief occasion, with the loukoum-eating mother and daughters on my right side, or with the young, heavily cologned couple on my left, was it not because I was a cultural tourist, something I could no longer afford to be in my own country?

Because, really, Farid El Atrache and Chadia were singing in Spanish, and I had always seen those oily foreheads and lacquered hairdos in Buenos Aires, any Sunday at the Boca stadium, or waiting by nightfall at the corner of Maipú and Lavalle; and the coy romance and broad laughter I was enjoying out of the Paris cold on my evening off *le quartier* were precisely the same that frightened me when they wore the faces of Palito Ortega and Violeta Rivas. It was really the undulating blue and white flag, the everlasting smile of Gardel reincarnated in that of Perón, the excruciating appeal of *mate con leche* and the ethics of *gomina* and ejaculatio precox that I was discovering, in the full pride of a reborn Empire, under the black and white Egyptian sun.

When the film was over, all the youngsters who had whistled in admiration at the modest display of shoulder and knee that Chadia's conservative bathing suit allowed, walked away in the night, indifferent to the huge naked ladies advertising the weekly renewed erotic demonstrations of permissive neo-capitalistic Europe. I had a mild shock at the shop signs and street names in French: because I felt almost certain I had spent a last, posthumous evening at the Armonia.

The Armonia was a shabby palace when I first visited it, sometime in the early '60s. But in the '30s, even in the '40s, it must have catered in all its stucco splendor to the respectable lower middle classes of the neighborhood. Coups d'état, perfunctory industrialization, monetary devaluations, demographic explosions, the advent of television, all left its wallpaper peeled, the original leather of its seats scraped and scrapped, an unassuming scent of urine reaching to the street. But the Armonia had discovered a way of prosperity in the unschooled audience provided by the railway station nearby. Soldiers and servant girls, whether inspecting the big city on a day's leave, or trying their luck on longer terms, rested their feet or enjoyed an unscheduled siesta while rainy visions of faded thrills barely disturbed the screen's surface. It was precisely this indifference to old, impracticable prints that allowed the Armonia to survive as a haven for lenient crowds and to become an early paradise of film freaks, who would find there items long out of circulation, though there was often little correlation between the titles hand-painted on the street billboards (posters being usually unavailable for such films) and the one unreeling on the screen. The fact that the Armonia did not advertise in the papers, its larger audience being of the kind that would not tell one title from another and just asked for a certain conformity to the most general patterns of entertainment, only enhanced its initiatic prestige.

There may be no record of the very first time that an old man's hand roved sideways on a soldier's knee, but by the time I started visiting the Armonia it accommodated a large number of teen-agers whose eyes would stay firmly on Kim Novak's breasts while their flies released a segment of their sticky inner life on the fingers of expert neighbors. The back rows of the theater were particularly prone to comings and goings whose nature it would be hard to explain by any notion of musical chairs. The short intermissions, though, would only reveal bored faces and clothes of no particular description, as if the spell of projected light, once discontinued, had returned the itinerant audience to the vacancy of a second-class waiting lounge. The Armonia could not choose with impunity such a transient clientele. The muted, somnambulistic animation of a decayed railway station was all it could afford in the way of glamour.

Already there and then I was a displaced figure, carefully scissored and pasted on the wrong photomontage. Fed on a steady, air-mail diet of *Cahiers du Cinéma*, I was there to get a glimpse of classical syntax and severe violence in some Budd Boetticher western I had missed on its, albeit inconspicuous, first release. I filed the heterodox couplings, the gasping and fumbling rehearsed in a voluble darkness, under that low reality unredeemed by the process of being recorded on a strip of celluloid and projected by a cone of axiomatic radiance on the screen.

Years later, when cinephilia already was for me but the memory of an outlived ailment, the old issue of an evening paper, inexpensively wrapping a pair of shoes I had had mended, told me in a flash of distraction that the Armonia had closed down after, though not perhaps due to, a police investigation into the death of one Ricardito Ordóñez, aged nine, raped and smothered in the men's john by a construction worker from the Northern provinces, who, after having won the child's trust with generous helpings of chocolate-covered peanuts, had coaxed him to the toilet as the battle sequence of *El Alamo* started. Having thrust the full extension of his desire between the tight, questioning buttocks of Ricardito, he proceeded to quell the inordinate wailing with his tattooed right arm, thus turning a gesture of passion into an unwitting feat of necrophilia. I visualized immediately the lighted sign reading Caballeros at the left side of the screen, and the occasional rectangle of light that would briefly expose the visitors on their way in and out, while a film was playing: another stage, unabashedly three-dimensional, where the action may have been off but could obviously be lethal, as opposed to the sustained, ketchup-smeared agonies on the screen battlefields.

Now I walked away too. For a moment I thought it was going to snow, the stillness of the freezing air a reminder of my present chosen surroundings. But it was not so. The stench of urine mixed with the rusty smell of the elevated tracks, the billboards had turned off their bulbs, and the Porte Dauphine-Nation line accepted me with a semblance of direction.

(1975)

The individual has been reduced to a mere succession of instant experiences that leave no trace. Rather, this trace becomes something hateful for the individual, because it is irrational, superflous, literally something "left behind". In the same way any book that is not new becomes suspect, and the idea itself of History (outside the specific boundaries of science) irritates modern man; thus the past becomes for him an object of anger.

In the civilized world, mourning becomes a wound, an anti-social sentimentality, because it shows that purely practical behavior has not yet been totally enforced upon man. . . . In reality, on the dead is inflicted what ancient Jews considered the most terrible of curses: Nobody shall remember you. In his attitude toward the dead, man allows his despair to burst out, despair at not being able to remember himself anymore.

Max Horkheimer and Theodor W. Adorno, "On the Theory of Ghosts" ("Philosophical Fragments" in *Dialectics of Enlightenment*).

(Painted Backdrops)

Palms for instance.

Unavoidable in tourism posters, they can convoke by themselves a dazzling sky like no combination of blue and yellow so far available in printing: a slight stoop to their trunks tells of the benign breeze, the unconcerned sway of their leaves conveys better than any choreography the casual bearing of tanned bodies by the sea.

They are meaningless, of course, unless enhanced as objects of desire from the industrial socialscapes of temperate cities. Each society dreams its doom, and the sun *is* that ill-defined circle of oily yellow among chemical greens and oranges, printed on paper and pasted on the walls of the Stockholm subway. It is available too: in Istanbul or Tunisia, in Ibiza or Rhodes, packaged with Swedish-speaking hotel personnel and round-trip weekly fares into a tour, itself subsumed in that stark burst of printed sunshine, in the black-on-white figures that spell its prize to welfare-state inmates.

Those are tamed palms, obviously. They may stand on an oasis beyond reproach, they may cast growing shadows on sand where the day's warmth lingers, but any erotic intercourse associated with their image has been translated into terms of a deferred exchange. Hard currency and underdeveloped economy stage now a play of rape, and only the willing suspension of disbelief in historical feedback stands for gratification. Though not transplanted, they are as alienated as the token palm trees at La Croisette, facing exhausted strips of sand once brought from a nature elsewhere, and dumped from trucks on the sea front.

It may be the expensive vicinity of boutiques and hotels, casinos and film festivals that keeps them alive. (Shorthand for them, dwarf potted palms have lost the phantasmatic tropic they may have projected once; blooming suddenly, like Japanese paper flowers in a glass of water, they propose instant winter gardens or breakfast lounges—the hushed, mildly obsolete glamour of names like the Ritz or Maxim's) If excised from that second nature, the one money can pay for, they would wither or harden, like the sturdy, yellowy, crusty trunks in the Plaza de Mayo, facing a government house painted pink, or their facsimiles in the duplicated greenery of the local Lake Palermo: yes, Buenos Aires palms are the saddest. Closer to the real landscape, closer at least than those in London or Frankfurt, they have been misprinted—they illustrate not the tropics, the gaudy laziness of Bahia or the polyglot, epicene fascination of colonies, whether Macao or Surabaya, but a no-man's land of displaced identity. Like the city dwellers, they belong to the zombie-like industry of some urban voodoo.

Maybe because they have always seemed to stand for something else, and to do so for somebody else, I find black-and-white, defiantly two-dimensional palm trees the most fulfilling, blinking, for instance, in back-projection behind cabaret girl and sailor boy-friend on their day off. There can be no exoticism in nature unless doubled by a social or cultural eroticism, they tell us, and it is the smell of the pineapple being cut in four, while I fumble for cruzeiros inside my wet bathing trunks, that spells Ipanema for me, as it is the labored typewriting of this sentence, watching rows of unrevealing windows from my own *fenêtre-sur-cour* that spells Paris for me.

Ras El Khaima, then.

I had never seen those words, at least together and in that order, when I discovered them printed under a pair of Comedy and Tragedy masks linked by intertwined ribbons, over an even more profusely ribboned lyre, all crammed on one side of a series of stamps. Such dramatic and lyrical effusion was justified by a brightly colored, minutely drawn picture on the other half of the rectangle. A bedaggered Othello, for instance, shrinks in terror at a limp Desdemona, both under a honey-colored canopy, with the words Verdi-Othello printed underneath, as a subtitle, on the 20 dirham piece. Thus, Gounod-*Faust* go with the 40 dirham stamp, Verdi-*Aida* with the 60 dirham one, Puccini-*Madame Butterfly* with the 80 dirham special, while Wagner-*Lohengrin* have been chosen for the 1 riyals command performance, and Mozart-*Abduction from the Seraglio* (*sic*, in English) reserved for the 2 riyals gala.

Having never been an opera fan or a philatelist, I was neither pleased nor outraged by the coincidence of those two passions—one for excess, therefore bound to extasis and stasis, the other for passivity, and therefore prone to connotative frenzy. In one of those reference works only the English dare publish, dauntingly titled *The Penguin Encyclopedia of Places* (of which the back cover states that the book's primary object is to answer such questions as "Where in the world is X?"), I found out that Ras El Khaima was one of the "trucial states," a group of seven British-protected Arab sheikdoms on the Persian Gulf, between Qatar, Muscat, and Oman, with a joint population of 180,200, of which one tenth are nomads. Unassuming information ("the coast was once known with some justification as the Pirate Coast") quickly replaced every fact on the safe shelves of fable from which they had been momentarily threatened to be dislodged.

Charmed by a style of illustration that called to my mind Lebanese film posters, the pictures on the lid of Turkish Delight boxes, or the illustrations of Washington Irving's *Tales of the Alhambra* in their Argentine edition of the '40s, I lingered to notice a much draped curtain folding on one side of the picture, a discreet reminder of the stage where those rich summing-up postures and stage props attained their epiphany. But the tiny, unmistakably Islamic, over-dressed, glossy figures also belonged on another stage—one where Liberia can issue stamps portraying highlights of Napoleonic history, where the best-known sights of Venice grace in full color a series from Burundi, where a lone skier glides down a snowy slope with Paraguay's flagrantly foreign name printed underneath, or Jesus Christ is made to reenact his evangelic career on an effort from Togo. Maybe they all inhabit the boundless limbo of collectors, bent over their albums in the self-sealed seclusion of Umeå or Cali, dreaming of the ever-elusive other.

Maybe nobody in Ras El Khaima has ever seen those stamps I discovered one winter morning at the Philatelists Corner, on the ground floor of the Bazar de l'Hotel de Ville, more attracted by the incongruity of this short-lived development of a department store best known for its hardware basement than by any possible promise attached to the stamps themselves. They have always failed to entice me, even when I walked by shop windows filled with tiny scraps of countries I had only read about, on my way to English lessons and back. Was it 1949? We would sing "My Bonnie Lies over the Ocean" before leaving, as the first evening papers filled the stands with the word of a man in shirt sleeves called Perón, saying that the railroads were now ours.

(1975)

A kind of playful instinct is sometimes stronger than hunger. If it were not so, there would be no shopwindows left, no law being able to keep them from destruction.

Joseph Roth, *Travel Pictures*

Consider that a lot of things are meaningless and everything means . . .

Karl Kraus, *Sayings and Countersayings*

(Shoplifting Casualties)

After having done the ground level of the Bon Marché, a leisurely walk among book-covered tables and shelves, cosmetics displayed like priceless pieces of Etrurica on museum stands, and the less manageable luggage and photography departments, Teresa had already stepped outside on the rue de Sèvres when a plainclothes, unmitigatedly detectivelike stranger asked her to follow him. She did. Moments later, having yielded upon a formica-topped desk the impressive first volume of the *Petit Robert* and a bottle of *Y*, vastly different illustrations of what her friends refused to consider opposite halves of her personality, she faced the prospect of listening to a fit of preaching from her hosts, gentlemen boxed in double-breasted suits and wearing line-thin moustaches. The pompous banality of the French turn of phrase—to do morals to someone—timely distracted her into a blissful linguistic limbo from where she rose, literally, to her feet, opened her legs wide, and, the summer absence of underwear coming to her aid, started to piss, as in a trance, on the threadbare moquette underneath. As dramatic effects go, the act was enormous and effective. After a moment of unbelief, both men, as well as a gaping secretary attracted from the adjoining office room by the dripping sound, proceeded to haul her out, with less moral indignation than physical outrage. She left behind, of course, both book and perfume, but was able to reach the metro before the idea of having been deprived of her identification dawned on her momentary captors.

Such stark operatic flair was completely lacking in Susana, whom a commonsensical, immensely practical outlook had always protected from impatient lovers and a literary vocation. Her gift for realistic improvisation, of a rhetorical but immensely believable kind, was best displayed one winter afternoon when, an intoxicating scent of success already approaching her nostrils, she was in turn approached by a smiling, not at all unattractive man on the threshold of Bloomingdale's, going over to the Lexington Avenue subway. "Sorry, Miss, but have you paid for that?" he inquired, motioning with his head to the fur coat nonchalantly cast over her right arm. She was quick and dazzling: "No, I haven't, and I want to see the manager." Her wide smile and enthusiastic gleam of eye put the young man rather off. To the manager, or to somebody standing in for him, she was taken, and upon seeing him enter the room, she rose promptly to her feet: "I assume you are the manager. Let me congratulate you. For two weeks I have been doing research for an article on big New York stores, and, believe me, this is the first time I have met a security service worthy of the name. I've been lifting just about everything, from chocolate bars to garden machinery, out of Macy's, Altman's, Lord and Taylor's, and I've been through hell, going back and replacing everything, unnoticed, even ignored, by the people in charge, if they exist at all. Please let me have your name. By the way, do you happen to have a photograph you could lend for publication? I would be only too glad to have clippings of the article sent to you . . ." Having, in the way of a casual aside, produced, conspicuously though unceremoniously, a journalist's card from Argentina and a valid, hardcover passport, the smile stayed on her face, flexible yet resilient, while the man searched for some way of approach that could take in its stride both possibilities—that of the truth, unbelievable but undiscardable, and that of a thoroughly polished act, possible but impossible to assume as a public-relations risk for the house. Some twenty minutes later, Susana walked out regally—without fur coat, but escorted by a precious wake of puzzlement.

Alfredo, instead, approached the whole business in a different spirit. Instructed by Dora and Sylvia that the best way to do it was to actually buy something, and leave with far more valuable articles in pockets (or, if he could produce the assurance needed for it, plainly visible in his hands), he tried at different neighborhood supermarkets, without actually daring to approach the cash register at the end of the road. Stage fright got the better part of him on several occasions until he finally decided to go ahead. In haughty defiance of the bored-looking uniformed attendants (but was not that yawn the well-rehearsed mask of sharp detection?) and of an inscrutable silver-haired noncustomer going up and down the aisles, he dashed with what he thought of as Zorro-like gestures from stand to register, whisking along several articles of which only one landed on the counter: a brilliant performance as ballet goes, though the formal beauty of the gestures was not matched by comparable benefits—in his pockets, once at home, he only found a tube of tomato paste and a small, ornate jar of minced shallots, while he had paid, in terrorized compliance with the figures shown on the register, for a rather large, unappetizing box of Droste's mints.

Moira, instead, never relinquished a certain cheerfulness even for the most spectacular feats of what was her special line—not concealing but displaying lifted articles. Out of Bergdorf-Goodman one busy Saturday noon, she walked away in full leather and silk splendor, having left at a corner of a dressing booth an unattractive bundle that fifteen minutes earlier had been her jeans and cotton T-shirt. Her intensely labile features, what a boyfriend had praised as everybody's favorite identi-kit, the remarkable pliability of her hair, dropping wildly on shoulders and back, or easily done away with inside a scarf with Hermes's name visibly displayed, produced for the benefit of unwary salesgirls the illusion of different customers on the prowl. A convincing forgery of Rumanian, done by contaminating her native Spanish with shreds of Latin somehow kept from a hasty passage through the Facultad de Filosofía y Letras in the late '50s, managed to see her to doors, lifts, or plain exits, wrapped in a smile that no amount of well-trained offers of help could stop or tarnish.

Raúl never operated on such a splendid level of stage conventions or valuable commodities. Every afternoon, at the Prisunic around the corner, he managed to stand in line before the cash registers with a thin plastic envelope of smoked salmon inside his jeans, and a small, round glass container of caviar in his back pocket. Slimness of course helped, as well as the unsteady weather that allowed a lean raincoat to hang over his shoulders without offense to verisimilitude. Overcoats were not so welcome, being unsafe by reason of their own lenient capacity—tinned lobster and deep-frozen eel, though unspottable, were nevertheless heavy and gave to such outside garments a certain bulk, all their own, that spoke of undeclared cargo. Flagrant but so difficult to question, the chorizo or the bunch of merguez, safely propped on the front of his briefs, aroused greedy looks on the lady behind the register, who never dared utter the disingenuous words: "What have you got there?" Through the years, Raúl managed to make both ends almost meet, and to stay in reasonable good health; yet, so much safety in (minor) crime does not go without a certain gruesome sense of being firmly grounded on rock-bottom territory. One afternoon, having emerged from the register lines and heading on the escalator toward the ground floor, he started to cry, unaccountably and vehemently. To the astonished silence of other customers and a few vacant salesgirls, he walked áway in full pathetic isolation, knowing perhaps that he would not be able to get out of Paris much else than the fair belt of *jambon de Westphalie* around his waist.

(1976)

Alongside decayed roués of dubious origin and with dubious means of subsistence, alongside ruined and reckless cast-offs of the bourgeoisie, were vagabonds, discharged soldiers, discharged jailbirds, escaped galley-slaves, swindlers, impostors, lazzaroni, pickpockets, bamboozlers, gamblers, maquereaux, brothel keepers, porters, literary hacks, organ grinders, ragpickers, knife grinders, tinkers, beggars—in short, the whole amorphous, disintegrated mass of flotsam and jetsam the French call la bohème ...

Karl Marx,
"The 18th of Brumaire of Louis Bonaparte"

(Babylone Blues)

Row after row the lampposts on the Avenue de l'Observatoire light up among quivering tree tops, and I think this shall not be the last time you'll find an excuse not to go back home and write. The day passed almost unnoticed, wrapped in the tender warmness of May, and you have already forgotten that insignificant, necessary tissue of phone calls, errands and interviews which used up your hours. You remember, instead, some of the breaks between those gestures that should have assured you work, money, perhaps security.

You're standing by a fountain whose rusty turtles untiringly spew ornate trails of water toward a central column. Some effete horses seem to try and break loose from it without endangering the terrestrial globe towering over the ensemble. The changing blue of the sky is so diaphanous that you can see as far as the haughty pastry of the Sacre Coeur as it, too, lights up for the evening. The scenery reminds you briefly of other, less pretentious turtles on a Roman fountain, of a more graceful church on a Florentine hill. You have learned, though, to feel at home among Paris monuments and in moments such as this, when the light of a certain hour of the day touches them with a fleeting grace, the city itself seems to accept its destiny of stage decor, painted backdrop in front of which too many characters from different plays or from successive productions of the same play, have fretted. The memory of those plots leaves the stage undisturbed, its possible magic being but a mirage of layered traces, of forgotten battles.

Yes, maybe tomorrow you'll be in a better mood to write. Today's comings and goings have exhausted your attention and it's precisely the fleeting complicity of this light that may appease your restlessness, that nameless impatience that eats you . . . (And yet you know nobody waits for you in those café terraces so full of conversation, that you'll recognize faces you'd rather not greet, that out of pride you'll not dial from a phone booth that number you know by heart, nor shall you yield to the welcoming promiscuity of darkening parks.)

An aging couple walks by you. They are quarrelling in very low voices, in a language you decide, on a whim, is Hungarian. The ageless clothes, the painstaking tidiness betray years of regular dry cleaning. On her lapel there is a heavy brooch, where a few stones are missing: the detail seems to tell less of bygone splendor than about a tenacious, superstitious clinging to a modest family heritage, some jewels that were never splendid to start with, maybe kept in a knotted scarf, or not: rather, in a sewing box turned jewelry case, bequeathed by an aunt, not at all on her death bed but on the eve of some war, or, rather, on one of those uneasy farewells emigration brings about . . .

Once more you stand at the numberless crossroads of bad literature. It doesn't matter—you embark once again, with a pleasure only a shade guilty, in that perversion of everyday life: what could have been, what could be . . . Humble, silent, live ivy or a damp stain, it proliferates in intricate, insignificant designs, vacant characters, passersby unaware of the plot you're weaving around them, of the past you inflict on them, of the future you may not care to invent for them. (On your table, darkness has arrived from the window and reaches the pages of your notebook, always blank.)

At the mercy of these open fictions crossing your path, you have wondered aimlessly. It is already night, gone is that elusive moment when electric light and the last gleam in the sky coexist in brief unreality. No Magritte retrospective, nor an abuse of film effects may wear out your taste for those minutes blurring the frontiers of day and night, when an insidious silence creeps among the traffic noises and interferes with the trading of voices, when your footsteps, your breathing, even your pulse suddenly invade your attention like brand-new objects of interest.

You realize that the coal store on the rue d'Assas has become a fashionable bistro, to the point of calling itself the Coal Store. A man tries to deal with the code of numbers and letters that should enable him to enter an apartment block. Nothing, nothing—pass on by—do not think about them, don't let your imagination alight on them. Why write if not to tell the extraordinary, to dare tread where a Karen Blixen story may espouse cheap fiction? "The Immortal Story" may be the only tale worth writing, "The Sailor from Gibraltar" the only one worth rewriting. Exotic harbors, wayward fortunes, errant Jews, nomadic women, sailors appointed to realize somebody elses's fiction or dismissed so that fiction may live its own free life. *Romanesque, Novelletish* . . . Where does the pejorative inflection creep in, where does the definition of desire vanish? Does it really matter?

In the daytime cities are different, by night their streets cross unexpectedly, rivers flow into each other, passersby seem willing to speak other tongues. Suddenly the high matrons on the Pont du Caroussel, the grandiloquent facade of the Gare d'Orsay, the trees on the lower embankment, hesitating by a dark stream which seems to vibrate without flowing—everything lights up with a spectral radiance, as if about to confirm your suspicions and reveal the glued cloth behind the house fronts, the cardboard of the tree trunks, the paper of the leaves. The honey-colored spotlights from the *bateau mouche* pass by and the decor is restored to a consolatory dimness. You start on your way again, other indistinct figures too. The blinding moment of danger has been conjured, the city and its people retrieve the part of reality they had. Your memories are to be displaced by the unwritten fiction walking by you. Your loneliness shall be erased by fatigue.

Back home you shall not notice the notebook on the table. It won't be a deliberate ommision: it won't meet your look, just like the TV dinner in the upper compartment of the freezer, or the key ring that deep in a drawer keeps the possibility of opening doors that no longer are those of your home or of your friends', in a city that no longer exists.

(1979)

Of these cities will remain only what blew through them— the wind.

Bertolt Brecht, *Manual of Piety*

Everybody knows these cities were built to be destroyed . . .

Caetano Veloso, *Maria Bethania*

(Fast Food)

1.

My father held spices in moral contempt: "If the food is wholesome, it needs none of that rubbish," or "They made sense at a time when people couldn't help eating rotten meat." He thus upheld, unwittingly, a domineering ideology in Argentine life, which the overgrown middle classes tamely absorbed from their betters. Such a painstaking confidence in the virtues of the noun, rather of a few nouns, suggested to me a no less tenacious mistrust of all modification, of the mere shade an adjective may instill. Version, perversion, inversion.

Such utterings did not prevent my father from enjoying vanilla in his custard, saffron on his rice, origan on his tomato. But beef and salad presided over his gastronomy with almost Mosaic authority. Even today, Argentine palates and noses not aspiring to snobbery refuse to enjoy garlic, socially ostracized by its connotations of immigrant poverty as well as by its capacity to render the body present in all its pores. An upper-class girl changes her Spanish itinerary and does not stop at an Andalusian village because it smells of garlic. A less flashy citizen is sorry his Genoese mother-in-law cannot do without garlic in her weekly lunch ritual.

2.

Rare, distant, disputed objects of desire, spices were to become money, taxes and justice weighed and paid in pepper. This symbolic capacity was to unleash crusades less bloody, more unremitting than those supposedly directed to free the Holy Sepulchre. As the centers of political power, following the capitals of commerce, displaced themselves westward, ever more intricate and adventurous roads toward riches were devised with ever renewed rapacity. Thus the Silk Road gave way to the Spice Route, Christopher Colombus succeeded Marco Polo, new and warring empires were built on the successive rubble of previous empires. Frenchmen and Englishmen festered on Dutch ruins, themselves once built by the Portuguese. Such empires, lofty and haughty fabrics of law and language, turned out to be no less fragile and perishable, their nature no less symbolic, than that of paper money, going from hand to hand like gossip, its only identity a mere convertibility.

(Clove and musk perfumed the wind guiding the ships. Malabar, Malacca, Bengal, Colombo, Martaban, Batavia . . . incantatory names of ports and factories announced those of the spice islands, the delicious Moluccae—Terneta, Motir, Timor, Makian, Matchian . . .)

If it's true that the American gold Colombus brought to the Spanish treasury would pay for the Hindustani spices Vasco de Gama discovered, the peppercorn, the New World's main contribution to the European palate, was to be dispossessed of its American identity as its original name was effaced: Latinized as *pigmentum*, vulgarized as Spanish, Turkish, or Indian pepper, from Calicuta or Guinea, East and West themselves confused in the name of those Indies for which a place on the map was found much after they became rooted in the imagination that feeds desire.

The conversation of slave traffic and spice trade brought that transatlantic pepper to the West African peoples whose descendants buy it today in the Belleville or Ménilmontant markets, no longer slaves but immigrant workers in the promised land of the European Common Market, their countries no longer colonies but Third World, the fiction of statesmen and intellectuals eager to export technology, diplomacy, or revolution, paying heed only to that fleeting nod History usually bestows too late and never for good.

New bosses, new names. Always: discover, cover, cover-up.

3.

I remember how, on the 18th of April 1974, between the Tribunales and Callao stations of the Buenos Aires subway, the fundamental hypocrisy of all ideological operations became apparent to me. While in the so-called capitalistic societies an idealistic image of history is fostered, protecting the social machine and its crass material operations from the unflattering public limelight (what schoolboy is given the fundamentals of banking or profit economy?), in the the so-called socialist world materialism has been enthroned as a philosophical fatum the better to enforce the rigid morality of a proletarian gospel, with History in the role of Redeemer and

110

Equality, that lusterless Golden Age, as its questionable reward.

I also remember that by nightfall on January 13, 1967, on my first visit to Berlin, I was moved as I recognized so many neon names: Bahnhof Zoo, Kurfürstendam, Marmorhaus, Fasanenstrasse, Kempinski. They were welcoming me into a fiction my memory had made up on its own, with cuttings from Isherwood and Döblin. (Next morning I would see for the first time the Wall and cross it at Checkpoint Charlie. I hadn't yet been in Kreuzberg, I hadn't yet heard a word of Turkish.)

Arriving at Lehniner Platz a smell of cardamom and unidentified frying assaulted me. Some men, who were not a group, seemed to move without leaving their places, shrugged and shuffled and rubbed their hands around a center of light and heat surrounded by snow: it was the first Schnell-Imbiss I saw, long before the today ubiquitous Macdonalds entered my consciousness, to be discarded after I became acquainted with New York's Taco Ricos. This one proposed goulash and shaschlik. Attracted by this humble incarnation of cuisines and phonemes that in Buenos Aires had donned an exotic prestige, as much as by such a sketch of social intercourse (itself no less untainted by literature) in the midst of the urban openness, I dared try one of those brochettes of supposedly Tartar origin whose popularity, like the hordes of their forefathers, stopped somewhere in central Europe. "*Curry oder Senf?*" A bulky, ageless lady, wrapped in a blouse stained in red and ochre, urged me to choose one of the sauces, smoking in metal containers, waiting for a plunge of the skewer holding bits of onion, pepper, and unidentified meat. "*Natur,*" I suggested, but her retort, swift and cutting, seemed less to answer back at me than to corroborate across the years my father's most pessimistic convictions: "*Natur gibt's nicht. Curry oder senf?*"

(1979)

111

"Cheerio," said the Baron with the air of one who makes a particularly felicitous quotation.

Christopher Isherwood, *Mr. Norris Changes Trains*

(Welcome to the '80s)

Rupert Holmes is singing *Him* and I, paper and pencil in hand, over forty years old, I'm trying my best to capture in a clumsy personal shorthand the words of the song, just as I used to, when I was thirteen, while listening to Nat King Cole or Johnny Ray. In this unexpectedly warm spring afternoon it feels as if I couldn't do without them.

I don't mind if, as you predict, Nostradamus's prophecies will come true earlier than reckoned and the world is to end in twenty months. I'm not impressed by not having to wait for the Second Millennium to gape at the pageantry of new cults and crowds in panic. I'm not shocked if Wojtyla's diminutive eyes, watery and yet so hard, have already seen Apocalypse and know that only Africa is to be saved.

It is pleasant to be in Madrid. I'm happy to discover there is an Andalusian rock, and day after day I postpone the return to Paris. From this indolent, benevolent city, which you like to call sub-Islam, I almost fail to realize that Barthes has died on us, and Hitchcock too . . . You tell me Henry Miller did not dare, either, tread on this decade. Suddenly we realize Sartre was alive because he no longer is . . . (Do you remember? *Littérature engagée*, keeping quiet about Soviet terror so as "not to throw Billancourt into despair," always running from manifesto to revolution, trying less to catch the train of history than to believe that nothing exists, neither Algeria nor Cuba or Vietnam, if the intellectual conscience of the sixth *arrondissement* has not acknowledged it . . . It's hard to believe it was only yesterday.

I ask you to turn off for a while the TV set, showering on us interchangeable images of refugees, Viets in Indonesia, Cambodians in Thailand, Cubans in Miami. It's been days since I've given up newspapers, where Chinese-Chilean solidarity vociferates almost daily, and as loud as Soviet-Argentine complicity. You tell me we're living in the post-Freud and the post-Marx, and I recognize a tone from my childhood —that of people speaking about the post-war, a space defined by an absence, not by content or desire.

Wars, however, whether in thunder or in uncertainty, always ended on a precise date, fixed by agreement or by exhaustion. We, instead, have started to realize this "after" once well into it. And this delay in perception, when we recognize it, leaves us more stunned than the simultaneous recognition of the new space of our survival. No flaming meteor alighted. Water did not turn black, nor trees into ashes. No seventh seal unchained prodigies and terrors.

If we look back, we can now read the scribbling on the wall, the telling scenes, a gesture where an uncertain agony may now be deciphered. However, none of them is definitive. More than cut, there was dilution. More than defeat, a fading away. Always, the humiliating feeling of having been blind to the revelation even while staring at it.

(Blind precisely because facing it? Blinded as by the light of dead stars, traces of a past life preserved by unthinkable astronomic distances, as the printed and projected image kept on film?)

Those who invested a modest intellectual capital in ideological speculation pretend nothing has happened. They may be waiting for an (unadmitted, unadmissable) cyclical return, which may grant them the dignity of prophets instead of the farcical charm of conned conmen. Others, less candid, hasten to shed all compromising evidence; they uphold an occasional syntactic ambiguity as proof of their heterodoxy, misprints witness to their irreverent humor, and without stooping to self-criticism they improvise the continuation of a revisionist discourse they never started.

No matter how amusing the display of opportunism, we are still restless—the air we breathe is not so clear as we might have hoped. It may be that the absence of (a certain form of) lying does not suppose the reign of (some form of) truth. Those of us who in the time of Freud and Marx preferred to take their word for an instrument instead of a system, individual openings instead of laws, as we now witness the rebellion of reality against letting itself be interpreted by that word, we feel less amused than we could have expected.

True: better to be in the open, without refuge, than sheltered under a policy of clean consciences, invoking justice to impose uniformity, turning health into a moral standard. Behind so many Potemkin villages which enlivened the hectic steppes of this century, there throbbed, however budding or

116

misguided, some ethical impulse. Today the scene has gone, undisputed, to those who never relinquished power, even more united now in the international solidarity of repression. Those who prided themselves on being more alert, less naive, piercing appearances to disclose hidden motives (the other side of the canvas, infrastructure, the repressed—metaphors all of different origin but equally devaluated because equally dependent on the mirage of surface and depth), now we face reality's answer: a shrug, perhaps a friendly laugh, underscoring a pitying glance. You realize only now? it seems to whisper, only now that for the winners of History there was never hesitation? That today, as it always was, maybe only more frankly now, there is no possible dialogue except between money and money, between force and force, between power and power?

"No one is gonna get it for free," intones Rupert Holmes. Our eyes meet and we start to laugh. It's already getting cooler. In an hour or two we'll be able to go out into the night.

(1980)

(One for the Road)

Today I feel like writing about Buenos Aires.

The saga of vanished wealth feeds on the swindles of History. When I first saw the Alexandre III bridge it was unfashionable to like it and, long before it became acceptable, I grew attached to it. I failed to see it only as the less arrogant, more graceful companion piece to the Grand Palais and the Petit Palais, its gilded garlands, majestic matrons and pompous *putti* charming remnants of the 1900 World Exhibition. For me, its rusty greens and grays preside over a ghostly assembly of Russian bond holders. Lulled by the legendary breadth and visible riches of an empire that, on such a cosmopolitan occasion, would present the city of Paris with a durable monument, a host of eager bourgeois subscribed to an issue of bonds launched by the magnanimous, friendly power. Wasn't the bridge at the same time fancy and solid?

The Soviet government, of course, would firmly decline to honor engagements of a regime it had abolished. The original holders, later their children, more recently a steadily dwindling number of their grandchildren, renew every so many years their claims at the International Court of Justice, in The Hague. In 1978, in a dilapidated *appartement bourgeois* in Passy, I discovered the original bonds, decorating in the way of faded wallpaper the children's room, probably feeding with their administrative small print a nocturnal, grim fairyland.

I used to imagine Manaus as a maze of run-down mansions and cracked-up boulevards around an upstart cathedral. Most often I pictured to myself the haughty Opera Theater—the yellow and white neoclassical Teatro Amazonas where Caruso sang on opening night—its original masonry now rusticated by cracks and chips, its moldering velvets embroidered by fungi and dampness, creeping jungle weeds insinuating themselves into the boxes, a stage set of lianas drowsily waiting for an unwritten score or occasionally visited by a coral snake from the orchestra pit.

Hadn't the city submitted itself as a willing stage for the wishful thinking of the Brazilian rich? Fed on the rubber boom that barely survived the First World War, its ruling reckless class was uncommonly helped by Nature to live up to

121

their imaginary characters: wasn't the Amazon the only practicable way of transportation, wasn't it easier, once on the Atlantic, to head northeastward to Marseilles or Genoa, even Southampton or Le Havre, than to try south, sailing around the obese coastline?

Thus, dry cleaning would be performed somewhere on the Mediterranean, while British tailors and haberdashers made their way up the river, to take measurements for custom-made goods to arrive by mail months later. A godfatherly, well-wishing British corporation built an impressive stone quay, capacious storing facilities, and, most spectacular, the floating wharves that would keep step with the unpredictable rises and falls of the river waters . . . Come the war, they also transplanted samples of the rubber plants to colonial Malaysia, where, under British rule, they grew healthily, judiciously, and profitably—to be transported and commercialized all over the world at dump prices, thus ruining the Brazilian economy.

I know, of course, that today Manaus has been reborn as a thriving state capital, but its university or the Trans-Amazonian highway entice me less than the visions of sleepy, unending decay my father had in 1934. I used to listen to his tales, some fifteen years later, with the same absorption aroused by his memories of earlier calls at Punta Arenas, once the final destination for boats sailing from Trieste and a far outpost of Austro-Hungarian trade. Its sumptuous hotels, opulent stores and Mittel-Europa whorehouses were struck dumb by the opening of the Panama Canal, which came to monopolize the greatest bulk of Atlantic-Pacific crossings. Such amenities slowly faded into the ever-shabbier garb of a Patagonian free port, only seldom graced by international traffic. By 1931, father told, the Sacher torte he had at the local Grand Hotel was stale, and a number of Chilote Indian girls were already boarded at Madame Crepusculescu's.

And what about Trieste itself, left quivering between blurred borders when the empire that backed its commercial splendor disintegrated into hopeful, short-lived democracies? And what about Alexandria and its polyglot miscegenation of greedy minorities, to be dispersed by the Islamic renaissance? They are on the map all right, and maybe among the brand-new housing developments and the all-native population a vestige of the old rapacious city may still be recognized. For me, however, their plots have thinned beyond retrieve. They remain cities of the mind—their cartographers are called Svevo, Saba, Cavafy.

Behind the splendor of great capitals I enjoy detecting a ghost town struggling to be released: to see in the facade not so much the extravagant shopwindows and dazzling lights as the moldering spot, a crack rich with menace, the desert underneath; to see through the assertive presence the impending shadow. Were it not for a resilient allegiance to ports, Rome would be my city, if only because it has evolved a modus vivendi amid its ruins. There, the dead and the living have perfected a mutual indifference during centuries of daily intercourse. Its riches are fragments of ever-renewed, ephemeral despotism, scraps of devaluated pride; before Mussolini's revivalist folly, they amounted to a haphazard decor where life was candidly conducted: archeologist and whore performing side by side, regardless.

I think it's the proper thing for ports to look away from the mainland they are supposed to serve. Imported goods are invested with the feeble/forcible magic of foreign language and exotic custom, and the exports paying for them are so many bottled messages sent out, yearning for unexpected answers, for sheer possibility.

Incantatory names: Lloyd Triestino, Compagnie d'Assurances de Trieste et de Venise, Banque de Shangaï et de Hong-Kong . . .

For years I repressed a guilty infatuation with this dubious literature of commerce. Later I came to accept it as an innocent side show in the Marxist canon. Today I feel like writing about Buenos Aires.

(1978)

Freedom is just another name
For nothing left to lose.

Kris Kristofferson, "Me and Bobby McGee"

Note

In the same way postcards seize and reproduce the most typical aspect of a landscape, a monument, or a face, these texts would like to manufacture common, public images, a *déjà vu* that would dilute whatever is too subjective in an individual's sensibility and experience.

The quotes linking and separating these postcards are residues of reading, a habit I find less and less fundamentally different from writing. To those found objects, other people's written words, I have entrusted the continuity of my own written words, the lighting, brutal or perfidious, of the text just read and of the other to come. I have written these postcards in English, a "foreigner's English" I later translated into my native Spanish, less because of autobiographical reasons or because English has been for me the language of literature, of the imagination, than out of desire to erase the notion of an original—so that certain turns of phrase found in translation would be incorporated later into the translated language, until the original itself becomes translation.

I would like to add that if the country of birth is often the Fatherland and the language mostly the Mother tongue, in these exercises of writing, reading, and translating, facing each other in the deforming mirrors of different languages, the exile speaking and spoken of is the son's.

Edgardo Cozarinsky

127